LIGHTS OF THE Heart

NAT BURNS

BELLA BOOKS

2016

T0127065

Copyright © 2016 by Nat Burns

Bella Books, Inc.
P.O. Box 10543
Tallahassee, FL 32302

All rights reserved. No part of this book may be reproduced or transmitted in any form or by any means, electronic or mechanical, including photocopying, without permission in writing from the publisher.

This is a work of fiction. Names, characters, businesses, places, events and incidents are either the products of the author's imagination or used in a fictitious manner. Any resemblance to actual persons, living or dead, or actual events is purely coincidental. The publisher does not have any control over and does not assume any responsibility for author or third-party websites or their content.

Printed in the United States of America on acid-free paper.

First Bella Books Edition 2016 ·

Editor: Amanda Jean
Cover Designer: Sandy Knowles

ISBN: 978-1-59493-524-4

PUBLISHER'S NOTE

The scanning, uploading, and distribution of this book via the Internet or via any other means without the permission of the publisher is illegal and punishable by law. Please purchase only authorized electronic editions, and do not participate in or encourage electronic piracy of copyrighted materials. Your support of the author's rights is appreciated.

About the Author

Nat Burns began her award-winning writing career as a freelancer, then later worked as a staff journalist for two Virginia newspapers.

She has often worked as an editor and still does. After suffering a TBI, Nat retired from her demanding editorial systems coordinator job at a Washington DC-based medical journal.

She is now a full-time novelist and this is her ninth lesbian romance for Bella Books.

In addition, Nat is the music editor for *Lesbian News* magazine where she has a monthly column called "Notes from Nat."

www.natburns.com
www.bellabooks.com/Bella-Author-Nat-Burns-cat.html
http://tinyurl.com/k9ayr5k

Other Bella Books by Nat Burns

Two Weeks in August
House of Cards
The Quality of Blue
Identity
The Book of Eleanor
Poison Flowers
Family Issue
Nether Regions

Dedication

I want to dedicate this book to all the hardworking physicians, medical workers, activists and volunteers who work with patients and families suffering through Traumatic Brain Injury (TBI). Their patience, tolerance and joy for living are unmatched.

Acknowledgments

I'd like to acknowledge the incredible help of Dr. Cynthia Cavazos-Gonzalez, a Texas neuropsychologist, who tested me extensively and helped me understand, and come to terms with, the idea that my new normal was just that—a new normal for me.

I wish to offer my eternal thanks to speech pathologist, Caroline Skill, for helping me to find my voice again.

And thank you, Barrett, my retired nurse writing friend, for advising me on certain medical elements.

I must also thank all the members of my local book club and the Petroglyph Guild for listening to me loudly work out plots during our get-togethers. You are good friends.

And, as always, thanks to Bella Books and the production staff there who keep me out of trouble.

Finally, importantly, thank you, Chris, for reading and rereading this manuscript (*te amo*).

Eres la luz de mi corazón, mi alegría.
-Corinthia Madsen Salas

PART ONE

CHAPTER ONE

Maddie

I liked to watch her. Sometimes I would leave my office door cracked a little so that I could observe her as she smiled at my patients, or frowned at a misbehaving computer program. Ella Lewis was beautiful. Oh, not in a classic sense—she was a bit too short at just taller than five foot, and a bit too plump in the middle. Yet I relished those slight imperfections. When I looked into her dark blue-green eyes, we connected somehow. I'd never experienced that before. With anyone. This was all new, and I wished desperately that I could explore it to the fullest.

I rose and stepped from behind my heavy wooden desk. I was restless, railing at an unfair universe that would show me my perfect mate then have her work for me. It was not fair dangling a carrot before a donkey and then binding its feet so it couldn't move forward. I sighed and studied the certificates papering the office walls. The wooden frames gleamed in the morning light from the street-side window.

The honors mocked me. Corinthia Madsen Salas, Doctor of Medicine. Corinthia Madsen Salas, Doctor of Humanities-Ideas thrown in just for fun. My eyes traveled across about a dozen other framed certificates—residency, adjunct residencies, citations of gratitude and of success. It was a whole wall of framed paper saying that I was a good and honorable person. I turned and peered through the opening that spotlighted the receiving desk out by the enclosed waiting area.

Ella was talking to my nurse, Sandy Webber, and she was facing my office door. I ducked back, just in case her eyes lifted. Shaking myself and straightening my short white lab coat, I laughed soundlessly, embarrassed by my childish actions. I glanced once more at the wall of success and then stepped into the hallway.

We had only two examination rooms as I was in a solo practice, and I was confused to see that neither room had a flag raised to indicate that there was a patient waiting inside. I peered along the hallway in a fog, perplexed for several seconds, and then reversed my direction and headed toward the front desk. Both women turned to me as I approached.

"Hey, Doc Maddie," Sandy greeted me in her usual boisterous manner. Ella hung back shyly, and I made a concerted effort not to look at her.

"I guess you're wonderin' where all your patients are today, ain't ya?" Sandy continued. "Well, there's been an oil fire over at the Hamburger House. No one hurt, thank the lord, but the firetrucks got Central all blocked."

I nodded, catching on. "So now everyone's going to the McDonald's outside town for their breakfast."

Sandy laughed. "You know it. Ceptin' for old man Travis. He's coming in for glucose so he'll be right on."

I rubbed my hands together to warm them. "And that means I have time for more coffee."

"Would you like me to get you some, Doctor?" Ella asked.

I shifted my eyes toward her and took a deep breath to calm myself. What was it about my new medical assistant that turned me into a bumbling teenager every time she turned those sultry eyes my way?

"Make sure it's two sugars and two creamers," Sandy said, shoving Ella toward the kitchen area.

I opened my mouth to say something, anything, but she was gone. The phone rang, and Sandy reached for it. I made my escape back to the safety of my office. Moments later, Ella tapped on the door I'd left ajar.

"Here's your coffee, Doctor Maddie. It's freshly made, just fifteen minutes ago." She smiled and approached my desk.

I cleared my throat and popped my reading glasses onto my nose. This made her image somewhat blurry so I was able to smile at her, take the coffee and carefully place it on the desk. "Thank you, Ella. I appreciate it."

"No problem. By the way, did you get a chance to finish the evaluation I left on your desk?" She tilted her head adorably to one side. I took off the glasses. I wanted to see her, no matter what.

"Evaluation?" I cleared my throat again, annoying myself and certainly annoying her.

She smiled indulgently, and I wanted to lick the dimple on her right cheek. "You know. The ninety-day evaluation? Sandy has to comment on it as well, and she asked me about it this morning."

I looked down. I had placed it aside. Ella had been with us ninety days. She was so efficient that it seemed as though she'd been here forever. I'd set it aside because I still agonized over fudging a bad review, just so she would go work elsewhere and give my libido some peace. Yet I realized in that moment that there was no way I could act in such a self-serving, untruthful way.

"I—I'm sorry, Ella. It slipped my mind. I'll finish it today and give it to Sandy."

"It's okay, Doctor. I figured that's what had happened." She turned toward the door, and my eyes dropped to her sweetly rounded bottom, wrapped in dark denim. "Drink your coffee before it gets cold," she said softly as she pulled the door closed.

I let out a shaky breath and flopped back into my high-backed leather office chair. Yikes! I lifted my coffee and took a deep sip. Perfect.

I worked on Ella's review until I heard a commotion in the hallway outside my door. Sandy was showing my first patient of the day to the exam room. I looked over the review and made sure I hadn't gushed too much about Ella. It was fine. I signed it with a flourish. This meant she would stay with us. It was okay—I was damned either way.

I carried the review and handed it off to Sandy as she passed. "Mr. Travis is in one," she said unnecessarily as she scurried by. I thanked her and lifted the folder from the pocket just outside the exam room.

Clark Travis, seventy-four years of age, was an established patient. Last year, he'd presented with high glucose and, after a high A1C, I'd started him on metformin and dietary changes. This was his third follow-up since then. Sandy had done a fasting finger prick that was one hundred and three, so it looked as though the meds and changes had done the job.

I opened the door and stepped inside.

CHAPTER TWO

Ella

Most of my past relationships had been with blondes, so it was strange for me to be so deeply attracted to Dr Corinthia Salas, a shy, reclusive Latina of Puerto Rican descent. Of course, I'd found out most of what I knew from Sandy's overblown office gossip, and really, I had to wonder how much of what she said was true. Yet I could see the Caribbean in Doctor Maddie, as we called her. Her hair was the ebony of the papaya seed, and her eyes were the warm brown of the tamarind. Her skin, though she worked almost unceasingly night and day, always appeared sun-kissed, and I often longed to sweep one palm along that smoothly tinted surface.

I stepped out into the slanted sunlight of a south Alabama evening and glanced back once, hoping to see her behind me. Just so I could have her for a few more minutes. I sighed when she wasn't there. I walked slowly through the small parking lot to my tiny Toyota and headed for home.

I wasn't certain Doctor Maddie even *saw* me. Or, if she did, it was as an employee only. After pondering this for hours, late at night in my bed alone, I had finally decided that she was the ultimate professional. Certainly, it would be unethical for a physician to carry on with the employees of her office. Then again, there was the lesbian issue. I wasn't sure if Doctor Maddie was out to her patients, although my gaydar had gone off at our first meeting three months ago. The rest of the country might be making lesbians their media darlings, but in somewhat conservative Maypearl, she might want to be safe rather than sorry.

I knew she was single, though. I'd surreptitiously asked several people in the course of general conversation, and there was no evidence of a partner, of kids or even of a pet, in her office. As I drove along the quiet Maypearl streets, I wondered once more about her history, an exercise I was familiar with. It seemed thoughts of her filled my waking hours. I knew she'd grown up in San Juan, Puerto Rico and Manhattan, New York, following her nomadic consultant parents from city to city. She'd gone on to graduate from Fordham University, Sandy said, and I had glimpsed her MD one day from a medical school in Texas. But other than that, neither of us knew a thing about her private life. I knew she loved coffee and had a weakness for good avocado on crispy wheat toast. It was her favorite lunch.

I turned into the parking lot of my apartment complex and slid into my assigned space. Tropical Towers was a good enough place to live. If you paid your rent on time, and didn't infringe on the other tenants, you were left alone. Just the way I liked it. Yes, I was a bit lonely, but I did have Julio, my enormous gray-and-black Maine coon cat. Said cat was waiting for me as I approached the door. Perched on the windowsill, he watched me with huge golden eyes. I waved at him, and he leapt down and, as usual, greeted me at the door with loud vocalizations, reporting the indignities of his day. I listened attentively as I made my way to the kitchen counter, relieving myself of my lunchbox and handbag.

"I know," I sympathized just as loudly. "It's so hard being you and being stuck here all those hours by yourself. I just wish I could be with you, darn it!"

He walked figure eights around my legs, displaying our solidarity.

"So, what's for dinner, little guy?" I opened the pantry door. "We have whitefish." I waited but got no response. "We have tuna and salmon." Again, I waited.

He moved closer and peered up at me. I looked down. "Hmm, there's chicken?" He meowed loudly and then purred, rubbing his cheeks against my leg. I opened the can of chicken cat food and filled his bowl. After watching him a moment, I grabbed a beer from the fridge and made my way to the den.

Here I had books. Tons of them, stacked vertically and horizontally on every available surface. I studied their beloved, well-used spines as though picking the best pastry from a lavish buffet. I spent time on each one, silently recalling the stories tucked within. This was a murder mystery set in downtown Los Angeles. The cop had done it. This one was about a dysfunctional family who finds love and acceptance on a yacht in the South Pacific Ocean. Oh, and here was Michael Crichton's work about nanotechnology gone wild. I stepped to a second rank of shelves and touched a book about the origins of interesting things, and then another about word origins. I was tempted to pull one down but realized suddenly that I'd read just about all my books numerous times, these trivia ones in particular. So which to read? I wondered what Doctor Maddie liked to read. Surely not medical journals *all* the time. Did she like fiction?

Warmth flooded me anew as I thought of her, curled on a sofa reading… What? A steamy lesbian romance, maybe? I strode to the other side of the room and allowed my fingers to drift across the spines of the many trade paperbacks arranged like little colorful soldiers tucked into tidy barracks. These amazing books, hundreds of them, shared the lives and loves of lesbians. Some were not so good, too predictable, but others were amazing and thrilled me repeatedly. All were dog-eared as I reread even the bad ones obsessively. I needed a twelve-step program to break my addiction. I sighed and pulled one of my favorites down—in it, an unhappy housewife finds love with a new neighbor. Perfect. I looked around the room as I settled into my favorite chair. I wasn't a housewife and didn't know my neighbors, but maybe, just maybe, I could substitute beautiful Corinthia for the housewife and I could be her loving neighbor.

Julio jumped into my lap, his tongue smoothing his fuzzy black lips.

"Ugh! Cat-food breath," I said as I settled him into my lap. Then, comforted by his warmth and by my heated romantic imaginings, I read.

CHAPTER THREE

Maddie

"I think I've got bugs," Mary Elwis said, calmly regarding me.

"Bugs? Hmm." I pulled my wheeled stool close so I could study her. "What kind of bugs?"

"Little boogers. Can't hardly see 'em," she whispered urgently.

"Mm-hm. Do they bite?" I asked.

"Oh, no," she insisted. "They just crawl all around on my skin."

"Does it itch?" I took her arm and raised her sleeve. I didn't see a thing, not even any evidence of inflammation.

"Sometimes," she replied as she studied the arm, along with me.

I peered more closely. "You've got a lot of freckles—"

I let out a yelp and jumped to my feet. One of the freckles had moved.

"Doc? You okay?" Mary asked, recoiling back from me.

I took a deep breath and fetched a loupe from my supply shelf. I lifted the sleeve carefully and hovered the powerful magnifier above her arm. There it was again—movement.

Ah, hell, I thought.

"Yep, Mary, looks like you've got bugs. Ticks. Those itty-bitty ones. Have you been in the woods lately?" I lifted my eyes to hers.

Her eyes widened. "Why, no, I'm too old to be traipsin' through them woods. I had to get my grandson, Ernest, to go out after Sheba the other day."

"Sheba?" I sat back and regarded her.

"You remember. Sheba, my border collie."

A lightbulb lit above my head. "You have several dogs, if I remember correctly, don't you?"

She smiled proudly. "I do. Four rescues boarding with me right now. I'm thinking about keeping the little terrier I call Jezebel, though. There's not much out there cuter than her."

I nodded. "Well, that's all well and good, Mary, but we need to do something about the dogs bringing ticks—bugs—into your house. When they lay there next to you, the ticks crawl from them onto you."

She stared at me in amazement. "But I thought them things only went after dogs and cats and such."

I stood and peeled off my gloves. "You're not their favorite food, but they'll hang out on any warm body. The problem is when they attach and start...well...eating your blood, they can let disease into your skin because tiny bacteria live in their mouthparts."

"Well, I'll be." She sighed.

I stepped to the exam room door and opened it. I peered around the jamb and saw that the hallway was deserted. "I'll be right back," I told Mary.

Sandy was at the receiving desk, filing charts. Ella wasn't there.

"Hey, Sandy, we got bugs in exam two. Can you get some tick pamphlets and then come help me do the exam?" I asked. "Where's Ella?"

"Post office, but she'll be back directly. Be right there," she said, neatening the unfiled stack of charts.

I turned and moved back to exam two. The patient was sitting exactly where I'd left her.

"Okay, Mary. Here's what we're going to do. My medical assistant, Sandy, is coming in to help you get into a gown. The reason for that is I have to see if any of the ticks have attached to you. We're also going to rub some cream on you. It's called permethrin cream, and it will help kill the bugs that are on your skin. I'm also going to give you two prescriptions. One is for the cream, which I want you to rub all over your skin every night before bed. The other is for an antibiotic, just in case one has bitten you."

I pulled the stool over and moved close to her. "Here's the bad part. You are gonna have to either give up the dogs or fence them in your yard."

She frowned at me, eyes wary. "Why? Having dogs ain't never hurt nothin'."

Sandy entered the room and leaned to fetch a gown from the lower cabinet.

"Normally, I'd agree, but there's some pretty nasty things out there right now. You've heard of Lyme disease, right?"

She nodded unenthusiastically, and I continued.

"Well, there is a handful more bacteria-caused diseases that can make you pretty sick. Letting the dogs run the fields and woods is just bringing it all home to you. You need to fence in the dogs so they stay in the yard, where the grass is shorter, plus you need to give them a tick bath, with a special medicated shampoo, about once a week in summer."

"Bathe all them dogs?" Her mouth was open, aghast.

I stood and grabbed her chart as I moved toward the door. "You'll have to get someone to help you. Your grandson, maybe?"

"He'll help you," Sandy said soothingly as she shooed me out the door. "And you'll get those dogs tick collars too."

I stood at the nurse's desk at the end of the hallway and entered all the pertinent information into Mary's chart, including my detailed instructions, in case she called in with questions.

"Hey, Doc Maddie." Ella greeted me as she passed by with my next patient, eight-year-old Austin Miller, his arm in a bright blue cast.

"Room one's best for him," I told her, trying not to look at her too directly. "I need a film, though. Can you operate the X-ray?"

"I sure can. Come on, Austin. Let's go take your picture."

They moved along the hallway, and I took a deep breath.

Moments later, Sandy stepped into the hall with Mary's clothing, held at arm's length, and went into the small laundry area. She started the dryer and then beckoned to me. We spent the next fifteen minutes going over every inch of Mary's body. I found two ticks attached, one at the base of her spine and another in the groin area. Both were removed by liquid nitrogen, and the crawling ones we lifted off with packing tape.

"Now, Mary. Seriously, this is important," I began as Sandy applied the cream. "You'll need to wash and dry all the clothes you wear when around the dogs as well as all the dog bedding. I want you to run them through the dryer first while everything is dry, to kill all the live ticks. Then wash and dry them again. All on the hot cycle. Also, do they sleep with you?" At her nod, I continued. "Well, you need to strip your bed and do the same thing. The dryer first, then lots of hot water. There's a spray I want you to get too. Get it in the plant section. I'll write it down for you. It's a harmless kind of soap that will kill them, so I want you to spray it around your bed and your house. And again, use the cream at night, take the pills once a day and do lots of washing of clothes and bathing the dogs. You got it?"

She nodded reluctantly.

"It's important, Mary. You need to check yourself every day when you shower too. See if there are any on you. The first couple days, you may want to shower twice a day until they get under control."

"Twice a day?" she said. I could tell she was overwhelmed and knew this would be an issue revisited several times before it was resolved.

"I know it seems like a lot, hon, but Doc Maddie is just trying to keep you healthy," Sandy said as she moved to the sink and stripped off her gloves. "You don't want to get a fever or arthritis, do you?"

I patted Mary's hand. "Get dressed, and we'll have the prescriptions for you up at the front desk."

I carried her folder to the receiving desk and made a few more notations. I grabbed my script pad and jotted out Mary's prescriptions. "This one is soap spray, OTC in the garden area. It's for spraying plants, but she can use it on her house," I told Ella as I handed them to her. "Maybe you could explain that to her?"

"Why? What's wrong?" Ella whispered, leaning close.

She smelled like patchouli today. Man, I loved patchouli.

"She has ticks from all the dogs she keeps," I managed to reply.

"Ah," she said, nodding her understanding.

I straightened my spine. "Austin ready for me?"

She smiled, and I swear the room brightened. "Yes, Doctor. The films are in the wall bin."

"Thank you," I murmured as I hurried away.

CHAPTER FOUR

Ella

"Damn! I can't believe I forgot that," Sandy muttered, staring at the calendar she held. She was sitting in her usual chair next to me at the receiving desk.

I looked over. "What's wrong?"

A fretful baby cried out in the waiting room, and Sandy glanced up at the child before speaking. "Doc has a speaking engagement next week."

"So I guess we clear her calendar," I muttered, pulling the oversized appointment book close. "Looks like you've already done it," I said, indicating the two blank pages in the book.

"Oh, I know," she replied, waving one hand. "And Jason, over in Theodore, will take her on call. It's just I always go with her, you know, to run interference, take notes in her sessions, that kind of thing."

I waited expectantly. Nothing else was forthcoming, so I sighed. "I think I can handle everything here. I've been here almost six months. Unless you want me to take that time off?"

She shook her head. "Oh, no, sorry, kiddo, not explaining rightly. Can you go instead? Lisbet's sweet sixteen is that weekend, and I really don't want to miss it. I just need you to go for me."

I frowned. "When is it?" I leaned to look at the calendar.

"Next week. Y'all would have to leave Sunday, and she would speak Monday morning. You'd be back here by late Tuesday. Think you can do it?"

Warmth washed across me. Three days alone with Doc Maddie. Hell yeah, I could do it. "Of course," I said. "And I just need to be her secretary-like, right?"

She nodded. "Right. Just follow her around and do whatever she needs. It's easy. You know how easy she is to get on with. I usually just make sure she has coffee and check that she has her notes before she presents. Most of the docs she'll be talking to all know her so she doesn't usually get too nervous, or anything."

She watched me expectantly, as if waiting for further commitment. I conceded. "It'll be fine, Sandy. Don't worry." I thought a minute. "Hey, do you know where Tropical Towers is?"

"Sure, I do. Why?" She raised one eyebrow.

"Would you go by and feed my cat for me? The days that I'm gone?"

"You have a cat? You've never mentioned having a cat." She watched me doubtfully. Did she think I was fibbing about having one?

"Yep, yes, I do. His name is Julio, and he gets fed every day after work. Would it be too far out of your way?"

"Aw, heck no. I go right by there. I live out Fairlane way. Just past." She smiled indulgently.

I breathed a sigh of relief. I didn't know many people as I was something of a newcomer to Maypearl, and I didn't want to pay for expensive pet sitting from a stranger if I didn't have to. "Oh, that would be great. I'll put out an extra litter pan so you won't have to worry about that, but if you could give him his wet food every afternoon Monday and Tuesday, that would sure put my mind at ease."

"What would?" Doctor Maddie said as she approached and handed me a folder.

Tiffany Bledsoe waved from behind the doctor as they stepped to the receiving desk. Doctor Maddie's nod to Sandy indicated that Tiffany only had a wicked cold, so Sandy just motioned her to the door. "I'll send you a bill," she told Tiffany. "You just go home and put that cold to bed. Fluids and rest, that's all that works."

Tiffany smiled gratefully as she elbowed the door to the waiting room.

I realized suddenly that Doctor Maddie was still waiting. "Oh, Sandy's going to feed my cat," I explained quickly.

"Ahh, you have a cat?"

I watched as Doctor Maddie's face brightened considerably. Was she an animal lover, too?

"Yes, he's a Maine Coon. Are you familiar with that breed?" I watched her, entranced by this transformation.

"I am. My friend, Carla, who lived on Sixty-Fourth and First, she had one. A big, gray striped one." Funny how her brown eyes could sparkle so intently.

"Well, mine is more black with a little gray striping. I named him Julio, you know, because I got him in July. He was the cutest kitten—"

"She's going with you to Dothan next week," Sandy interrupted. "I hope you don't mind, but Lisbet, my Cynthia's girl, is havin' her sweet sixteen Sunday, and I promised her I'd be there. We're having a big to-do at the church and everything."

I watched as Doctor Maddie's face fell, and her eyes dimmed again into a business-like cast. I hoped it wasn't because I would be the one accompanying her to the conference. What if she thought I was a stalker and didn't want to be alone with me?

"No, that's fine, Sandy. I'm sure Ella will be good company." She gave me a brief smile before disappearing down the hall.

"See? I told you she'd be just fine about it," Sandy said. She turned as the outside door opened and a patient walked in.

I wondered who she was trying to convince, me or herself. I felt a laugh burble up inside me as I double-checked Tiffany's folder to make sure everything had been entered correctly. I ran a fingertip across Doctor Maddie's hastily scrawled notes. Her strokes were so forceful. I shivered just a little as I recognized the strength of her hands.

Three days with Doctor Maddie. I pulled the folder close, hugging it briefly before I turned to the filing cabinet.

CHAPTER FIVE

Maddie

The city of Maypearl had owned Dr Richard Pembroke's house since his grandfather, Tyler Pembroke, had been the first official family physician to set up a practice in Maypearl. The house purchase, by the town, had been a gift to that first Pembroke to welcome him to Maypearl. I always felt as though there was a little bribery involved, as well. Maypearl, Alabama was a backward, rural township of less than one thousand people. On a good census year. Not a big selling point for an up-and-coming physician. I didn't mean to imply that the people weren't great, they were. Salt of the earth, as they said here in the South, and that might have been why that first Pembroke had decided to stay.

The house had passed down through Tyler's physician sons and grandsons for almost two centuries, but then Clayton Pembroke—Richard's brother and only surviving relative, a building contractor in Dallas—had decided that he wanted no part of doctoring, or of Maypearl. He'd moved away, and that left only Richard to carry on.

Luckily, I'd met Richard at a conference in Dallas when I was a family practice resident at UT Southwestern. The conference was about unusual cases found only in family practice careers—a recruiting venture, to be sure. I fell for it, hook, line and sinker, as I had already committed to a family practice specialty. I just hadn't known where yet. Richard and I met at a group table of residents and doctors, and after copious wine, fettucine marinara and garlic bread, we'd decided I was to be his apprentice upon finishing my residency. He had never taken the time to marry or have children, preferring his studies and patients rather than a family of his own, so his practice would die with him unless he could hand it off to someone deserving.

I had spent six years sharing the practice with Richard, living in a small apartment off Cottonwood, but when he'd died plugging in a blender with wet feet during a pool party, the city had kindly offered me use of the home as long as I stayed on as Maypearl's doctor.

It wasn't a bad gig. I'd discovered that my college sweetheart, Amanda Sarious, had only wanted a busy MD so she could balance numerous affairs on the side, so leaving Texas had been a good thing at that time. The house they had provided was spacious, almost too much for one person living alone. A lot of nights, I fell asleep in the cozy den, on a daybed set into an alcove near the gas fireplace, even though I had a lovely bedroom upstairs.

Now, as I drove my Honda SUV into the driveway, I admired anew the impeccably landscaped front yard. Thankfully, George Niles, a retired gardener, had offered his services to the town for a small stipend. He even grew a vegetable garden out back, and I was eternally grateful for that. I was able to have fresh vegetables and berries all year round without having to lift a finger.

I was also grateful for Lilly Marsh, who cooked and cleaned for me. She'd left lights on downstairs, and the house looked welcoming in the steamy twilight. I grabbed my bag and stepped into a cacophony of frog calls from the wooded stream just west of the main structure. I smiled. What a great way to end a busy workday.

One of my favorites, lentil soup with lots of carrots and celery, rested on the back of the stove, and rolls still warmed in the oven. I shook my head as I fetched the salad and dressing from the fridge, along with a small pitcher of fresh tea. God, how I loved that woman! She'd even set a place at the table, so I seated myself quickly and dug in.

As my stomach filled and warmed with the delicious food, my thoughts strayed, as usual, to Ella. I had avoided thinking about the upcoming trip, but now, alone and safely ensconced in my home, I could let my fear run rampant.

I could easily predict how gut-wrenching being alone with Ella in a car for two days would be. How distracted would I be as I tried to present sixty minutes about lessening the fear of vaccines for babies, youths and the elderly?

I wondered if she would mind being with me. I wasn't the most engaging conversationalist, a fact pointed out many times by my ex.

I stood and carried my empty bowl and glass to the sink. I leaned against the counter and stared at the plain white café curtain that covered the window behind the sink. White. I turned and looked around the kitchen. There was nothing personal there. At least, not personal to me. Lilly had added a lot of nice touches, but they meant nothing to me. Turning back to the sink, I frowned as I rapidly washed the dishes and put the remaining food away.

I stood in the hallway. White walls, blank, no pictures beyond what had already been installed in the furnished house—and they were landscapes, mostly, with a few generic portraitures. I strode into the den and felt comforted. My books were on an end table. My mother's crocheted afghan was folded neatly on the back of the easy chair I usually sat in. My older briefcase stood sentinel next to that easy chair.

I thought of my bedroom upstairs, about the dull clothes in my closet, the simple toiletries on the bathroom vanity next to the sink. And I shrugged. I could not change who I was. I had been in school for a very long time and had never taken the time to build a life other than medicine and advanced learning. How could any normal person find that interesting? How could any normal person find *me* interesting?

I sighed and lifted the TV remote. After kicking off my shoes, I curled in my chair and comforted myself with my mother's afghan. I switched on the TV and watched the local news as my mind wandered.

I thought wistfully about my mother, Esperida, who I'd had moved here from Brooklyn when I'd decided to stay in Maypearl. I usually went every Saturday morning to visit with her, and I was glad we weren't leaving until early Sunday. Though it was only a five-hour drive to get to Dothan, I wanted to be there in time to settle in for Monday's early presentation. I'd go see her the Saturday before I left, even though she would not recognize me. She often thought I was her cousin, Paola. Tonight was one of those nights when I really missed my *mami*. The *mami* she had been before, fragrant and beautiful, full of life and fun.

Remembering my mother, how she had been before Alzheimer's had stolen her away, was painful. I was actually glad that my father had not lived to see her this way. And that he had not been left alone, as I had been.

CHAPTER SIX

Ella

I loved southern Alabama, and I especially liked the town of Maypearl. Claimed from the gulf shore in 1882, a fishing industry had quickly led to an established settlement. It was now just a small town, the fishing industry gone the way of huge commercial ocean trawlers. Yet the town limped along, businesses surviving by providing for human needs and desires. The residents went out of town for factory work, at the Kleune Refinery, thirty miles north on the Mississippi border, or resigned themselves to minimum wage work at the local establishments.

Driving to work, I passed a large grocery and a strip mall offering clothing, a tattoo parlor and a smoke shop. There was also a huge furniture warehouse and a Walmart shopping center with a doughnut shop and a juice bar. Then there was the Four Winds Mall, with its fancy name-brand stores. Oh, and there were two competing drugstores that always seemed to reside on opposite corners from one another.

Living in Maypearl was very different from my life on the Kirtland Air Force base in New Mexico where I'd spent my high school years. My father had been stationed in Germany when I was very young, and I had grown to love Europe with its sense of age and mystery. I dreamed of going back there someday. Then we'd ended up in New Mexico. Not a bad place, but though the people had been warm and welcoming, it was very different from Europe, being somewhat raw and new. The history there was all about the Native American, the fierce pueblo peoples who wrested some type of civilization from an unforgiving desert. In Germany, history was very different, focusing on the music of cathedrals, fine arts and centuries of ancient architecture. In addition, food and drink portions had been small there, relished with others in quiet surroundings. Meals in New Mexico had been huge affairs, riddled with hot or mild chile, and eaten surrounded by groups of people. Unique people, each shaped into a different character by the wind-battered frontier.

I pulled into my slot at The Chase Building where Doctor Maddie's practice was located. I looked at the sedate one-story brick building. Now, Maypearl was a different coin altogether. Steeped in Southern tradition, the townsfolk, though eclectic and oftentimes unusual, knew the boundaries of diplomacy. And what properly fit into right and wrong. I guessed moving here had been a subtle poke at my parents. They fervently believed that there was no place in the world for the sin of lesbianism, and moving to Maypearl was a chance to prove that I could be accepted anywhere.

I sighed and slid from my car. It was a plan that might have backfired. I'd been here the better part of a year now and had yet to meet anyone open enough to share a life with me. That stung a bit, but it was even worse because I now knew exactly who I wanted.

The object of my desire was getting out of her own car, a large, dark SUV. I glanced at my watch, surprised at her late start. Usually, she was in the office way ahead of any of us.

She beat me to the door and smiled over her shoulder at me as I approached. "Good morning, Ella. How are you today?"

I noticed the circles under her eyes right away. Was she troubled? Or just restless?

"I'm good, Doctor. How are you?"

She paused with the front door ajar, and I almost bumped into her, thinking we were moving forward. "Ella, I think that, since your probationary period has finished…" She paused and cleared her throat. "I think we should be, ah, a little less formal. I think that, I mean, when we are alone together, no patients, I think you should call me…call me Maddie, please."

I sucked in a quiet, deep breath as my heart thrilled. I managed to keep my voice calm. "Of course…Maddie. Thank you."

She nodded and preceded me into the waiting room. I shut the door as she made her way quickly through the receiving door. I turned on the waiting room lights and changed the sign on the door, letting Maypearl know we were open for business. I hummed a silly tune as I worked, my handbag and lunchbox still draped over my arm. I passed through the receiving door and went to my station at the desk. Just then, Sandy entered, and I knew my quiet time of glowing pleasure had come to an end.

"Have you pulled the patients for the day?" Sandy asked as she bustled into the receiving office and partially opened the tall sliding glass window that led to the waiting room.

"Not yet," I responded, dropping my bags and heading to the filing area. "Just got here, myself."

I checked the master list posted on a clipboard by the entry and began pulling patient files. I was finally able to put names to faces and was excited to see that Abby Hamilton was coming in at ten. Abby was a terminal cancer patient who had been released to hospice, and Doctor Maddie was following her palliative care. Abby, though only twelve years old, had taken her tragic diagnosis with Zen calm, and she radiated that calm and peace to all who encountered her. Her mother, Caroline, certainly destroyed by losing her only daughter, had become Abby's stoic anchor, and we had all fallen in love with both of them almost immediately.

"Abby's coming in," I called to Sandy, though she had been the one to compose the list.

"I know, I can't wait to see her," she said quietly. "It's been two weeks. Caroline sounded frantic. Not sure what that means."

I frowned at the files I held as my joy diminished. I didn't know if I was ready to deal with Abby in trouble.

I pulled six other files, wondering at the light load. Usually, we had eight or ten lined up this early in the day. I heard the bell on the front door sound, and I took the folders to the desk and stacked them neatly in the upright holder.

"Hey there, Danny. You don't look so good," I said, frowning in concern as I took in Danny Matthews's haggard appearance.

"Hey, Ella, I ain't worth much, that's for sure. Can't work or nothin'. Glad it ain't huntin' season or I'd be really pissed," he said. "Excuse me, ma'am," he apologized for his language as he nodded to Sandy.

Sandy waved his apology off, and I grabbed his file from the upright. "Come on back, Danny. Let's get you settled in."

I glanced back at his wife, Anna. "You gonna wait out here, hon?"

She nodded and lifted a library book. I smiled and nodded my acknowledgment. Anna was an avid reader, for sure, and I wondered anew how Danny, who obviously had no time for books, had snagged the tall, Amazon-like reader.

CHAPTER SEVEN

Maddie

I checked the chart outside the door, and alarm bells jangled along my nerves. Danny Matthews was a strapping thirty-three year old. There was no reason for him to be suffering from crippling diarrhea that he claimed had persisted for more than a month. He'd also lost too much weight. So many possibilities ran through my mind, not the least of which was cancer or someone poisoning him.

"Get a grip," I muttered to myself. "It's probably IBS."

I opened the door. Danny, a tall, burly man who usually weighed more than two hundred and eighty pounds, sat on the examining table. I looked him over as I shook his hand. His eyes were sunken, proof that he was not resting and that he was obviously dehydrated. Taking a deep breath through my nose, I determined that there was no smell of alcohol on him, so it probably wasn't due to chronic alcoholism, which could lead to diarrhea. Not that he'd suffered from that disease in the past. I took a seat at the little work surface and reopened the chart.

"Well, Danny. I see you've lost more than twenty pounds this month. That's not good." I turned to face him.

He smiled tremulously and spread his hands. "Well, Anna said I needed to lose a few," he joked. I could see his underlying fear and wished I had the wherewithal to reassure him.

"Not the healthiest way," I said as I pulled a diarrhea history template from the stack of forms on the clipboard from the hook next to my work area. "Let's see if we can get to the bottom of this. These questions may seem kind of personal, but they're important if we're going to help you get better. Okay?"

I waited for his nod.

"So, you said this has been going on for about a month? Is there anything that you can think of that might have contributed to this? Started it off?"

I could see he was really thinking it through. Finally, he shook his head. "I'm sorry, Doc. I just have no idea."

I hastened to reassure him. "That's okay, Danny. It's not unusual for this kind of thing to be a mystery."

He returned my smile even as his hands rubbed his thighs nervously.

"So, tell me this. Have you changed anything in your diet recently?"

He shrugged. "No, eat pretty much the same. I'm eating a little less 'cause I don't wanna be runnin' off to the bathroom all the time, though. Maybe that's why I'm losin' the weight."

"Hmm, could be. So you're eating…?"

"Well, burgers, roast beef. The wife has me on chicken three times a week. Says it's healthier."

"And vegetables?" I frowned slightly.

"Oh, sure, sure. Potatoes and peas and stuff. Carrots." He shifted uncomfortably.

I smiled again as I checked to make sure the whites of his eyes were clear. "So, you've never had a reaction to any of these foods before, have you?"

He fiddled with the front ties of his gown. "No, no. Been eatin' this way all my life."

I sighed, mentally ruling out irritable bowel. I made a note on the template. Next on the list. Artificial sweeteners.

"You say you've been trying to lose weight. Have you been eating any diet foods? Diet sodas?"

"Lord, no." He chuckled, seriously amused by the question. "I told Anna no way on those. I hate them diet sodas. Taste like medicine to me."

"No diet or sugar-free candy?" I watched him closely.

He shook his head. "I ain't much for candy of any kind, Doc. I have a nut bar every now and again but not much candy at all."

I made a notation ruling out a sugar-alcohol reaction. These questions were to determine whether his diarrhea was in the category of watery, fatty or inflammatory as each had its own treatment plan. So far, so good.

Next, sexual congress.

"Don't you get mad about this, but I have to ask. You and Anna have a pretty normal sex life, correct? I mean, no anal play, or anything like that?"

We both blushed as I awaited his response.

"Gosh, no, Doc. I'm pretty old-fashioned when it comes to, you know, sex."

"So, no contact with other men either?"

He looked horrified. I checked the no box and continued quickly.

"Does bread bother you? Or cereal?" I asked, crossing my legs and laying the clipboard on my knee. I studied him as he answered.

"I don't think so," he answered thoughtfully. "Though it seems like everything I eat sets this off, Doc. I even tried some of them medicines like pepto and that over the counter 'modium stuff. Didn't even touch it," he added.

I made another note. "It hurts, too, doesn't it? The gas and bloating?"

"Well, yeah. And my bottom is raw, to boot. It's just awful," he admitted. "Awful."

I studied him again. These symptoms were too soon to be something like amyloidosis, and he wasn't presenting with any of the other symptoms. He was a regular patient and his baselines had all been normal before this, so it likely wasn't anything congenital. He'd always been clear on STDs and HIV, and he hadn't been out of the country.

I double-checked. "You haven't been on any cruise ships, have you? Or out of state?"

"Nope." He spread his hands again, showing his helplessness.

I nodded and continued to study him with my eyes. He squirmed under my scrutiny, but I could tell it was discomfort. Not subterfuge. I looked back at the list. Parasites were next.

I tried to take a mental step backward, a diagnostic tool I'd been taught by Richard. "*Look at the big picture*," he'd told me often. "*It's crucial to family practice.*" A silence fell as I let my mind wander across Danny's life.

"Anna told me a couple months ago that you'd been away. On a hunting trip."

He nodded. "Oh, yeah. Me and the boys go up little Tombigbee every fall. There's a ranch we like up there. We always come home with a deer or two."

"Any beaver?" I leaned forward and supported my chin in one palm.

"Randy Coltraine got one up there one year, but I ain't caught none. Can't see goin' after killing beaver. I just go with deer, sometime squirrel," he answered indignantly.

"And you cook the meat all the way through before you eat any of it, right?"

"Yes, ma'am, Doc. My daddy warned me about that. He says some wild animals have diseases in their blood. That's why we drain them deer all the way too." His tone was proud.

"How about fish? You cook those well done?"

"Yes, ma'am. I don't care much for that sushi." He smiled at me, and I smiled back as something niggled in the back of my mind. I glanced down at the sheet. I stood slowly and set the clipboard aside.

"Well, Danny, let's have a quick look at you," I said as I pulled on gloves.

I slowly palpated his abdomen to make sure there were no masses. I checked his lymph system. His entire system was definitely irritated, but he still seemed in good shape. I decided not to subject him to the embarrassment of a rectal exam or stool sample.

"Okay, my friend." I helped him sit up, noting the trembling weakness of his arms.

I pulled off my gloves and took my seat again. I made an entry onto the diarrhea diagnostic sheet and then pulled off that top sheet from the clipboard. I slid the page into his folder before I sat back and addressed him.

"You need to promise me one thing."

His eyebrows raised. "Yeah, Doc?"

"That you will always, I mean *always*, pack in enough fresh bottled water for the whole trip. There will be absolutely no drinking of river or stream water and no washing of any food there either. And you need to tell all your hunting and fishing buddies about it."

"Yeah, yeah, I will. But why? What's wrong with the river water?"

I opened a drawer in my work surface and fumbled about. I pulled out a pamphlet and opened it. I stood and showed it to him. "See this little bugger here? I believe this is your new best friend, *Giardia lamblia*. It lives all over and especially in water around beaver. Sometimes it goes dormant, into little eggs, cysts. When these get inside a nice warm body like yours, they hatch out and cause all kinds of havoc. Or you may have ingested one of the little swimmers in the water and it proceeded to reproduce inside you."

He lifted his eyes and stared at me, a look of shocked disgust on his face. "These…these *things* are living in me?"

I nodded sadly. "A big bunch of them, by now. If it was a mild infection, your body would have fought it off by this time. Yours is pretty, well, persistent."

Abject terror crossed his face. "You gotta get 'em out, Doc. You can do that, right?"

I patted his shoulder. "Relax, Danny. No need getting yourself all upset about it. It—"

A soft tap sounded at the door. Ella stuck her head in. "Doctor Maddie, sorry to disturb, but Connie Wells is waiting outside for these scripts. Can you sign off for me?"

"Be right back, Danny," I said as I gently extricated the pamphlet from his clenched hands. I stepped into the hallway

"Is Danny okay?" Ella asked, eyes searching my face as I signed off on Connie's regular blood pressure meds.

"Remind her that it's only for one month and make her an appointment to come in for renewal. Danny's okay. It's Giardia infection. Caught it sort of early, so we will be able to deal with it successfully. Can you print off some generic stuff from the web for him? Make sure it's nothing too nasty. He's a little freaked out. But his wife needs to know how to keep herself from being infected, if she's not already."

I handed her the prescription printout absently as I turned, and my hand brushed against her soft, firm breast. An unexpected shock passed through my body and electrified the tender flesh between my legs. I know I blushed four shades of crimson. I was about to mutter an apology, but she thanked me breezily and headed back down the hall. I stood with my hand on the doorknob for a few seconds composing myself before I reentered the exam room.

I took a deep breath and smiled reassuringly. "So, Danny, what we're going to do is give you a prescription. This drug should knock them out of you and kill all the parasites. You're gonna have to take it every twelve hours for about ten days."

I pulled out my old-fashioned prescription pad and started writing.

"The worst part of all this is you can have absolutely no alcohol for ten days, not even a beer." I glanced sideways at him. "Can you do that?"

He looked eager. "Sure, sure, I can, Doc. If it'll kill those *things*. Oh, yeah, I sure can."

"Okay, good. I've got Ella printing some stuff out for you and Anna." I turned and looked at him square on. "She can get this, you know, so you've got to be really careful for a while, especially as you'll be expelling the cysts. Most will be dead but, well, we just want to be really careful. Wash your hands a lot, and use bleach to clean the toilet every day. I'll see you back here in two weeks, and we'll see where we are then, okay?"

I stood and shook his hand again. "Get dressed now and head to the front. I'll have your chart right up there."

I closed the door on his profuse thanks and hurried to my office. I set his folder on my desk and walked into my bathroom. I washed my hands slowly, relishing the sleek feel of the soap on my hands. I imagined it was Ella's smooth breast I was touching, and my breathing deepened as my body became fully aroused. I switched off the water and buried my face in a wad of paper towels.

CHAPTER EIGHT

Ella

"God, I'm gonna miss her," Sandy said.

I looked at her with surprise, but I had to concur.

We'd just helped load Abby into her mother's car, and both of us were feeling the sadness about her obvious decline. She was a fragile outline of what she had been before. Her failure to eat had brought her and her mother in to see Doctor Maddie, and her thinness had given her a translucent quality. Abby and Caroline's sad departure told us way too much.

Doctor Maddie stood at the receiving desk, making notes in a file. She glanced up at me briefly, and I saw that her eyes were red. Compassion swelling within me, I laid my palm against her back for a handful of seconds as I followed Sandy to our stations at the receiving desk. I felt her back stiffen and quickly removed my hand, worried that my touch had been too familiar. I had enjoyed the brief connection, wishing it could have lasted longer.

I took my seat between Sandy and Doctor Maddie, but just as I settled in, there was a commotion at the outside door.

"Oh, God, Doc, you've gotta help him," Blazeon Hughes cried out as she pulled her son, Chris, through the doorway. Even from behind the glass, I could see the blood darkening the T-shirt around his midsection. Doctor Maddie leapt into action and raced into the waiting room.

"Lift his legs," she barked out, causing Blazeon to recoil and obey. As a trio of horrified patients watched, Doctor Maddie lifted Chris under the arms and moved the three of them through the interior hallway and into the closest exam room. Sandy and I followed, and Sandy jumped into action, using surgical scissors to cut Chris's T-shirt off. I took Blazeon by the shoulders and led her to an out-of-the-way corner of the room. She was breathing heavily, sobbing, her breath a loud bellows of sound.

"Oh, Christ!" Doctor Maddie muttered as she saw the wound. "What the hell happened, Blazeon?"

"He was stabbed," she cried out, sobbing.

"I can see that," Doctor Maddie said with uncharacteristic sarcasm. "Ella, call a transport. He needs to go in."

I nodded and fished my cell from my pocket.

Chris was flailing his arms, hovering at the edge of consciousness. Doctor Maddie evaded his grasp, reached into an upper cabinet and drew out a surgical kit. Sandy wiped the abdomen with large surgical gauze squares to clean off some of the blood and then doused the area with dark brown iodine solution. Doctor Maddie ripped open the kit, drew on the nitrile gloves and opened a smaller suturing kit.

Blazeon whimpered, and I tried to get my arms around her. She was a large, tall woman, formidable to try to hold. "Shh, we'll help him," I said.

Doctor Maddie peered into the wound and then extended the surgical thread with a hemostat clicked onto the curved needle. "Hand me the benzocaine," she instructed Sandy.

Sandy fetched the already prepped syringe from a top cabinet and passed it to Doctor Maddie. Doc glanced at Chris's face and then inserted the numbing agent at several points around the three nasty-looking wounds. I winced, amazed anew at the things Maddie could do in the course of her job. As we watched, she examined the wounds closely again and then slowly sutured each one. On the lowest one, closest to the waist, she sewed two layers of tissue before inserting a length of pink rubber tubing from the kit and loosely stitching it in as a drain. With a final snip of the scissors, she stood back and straightened her spine. "Well," she said. "I guess that will do, if they give him a round of IV antibiotics and plenty of time to heal. Sandy, make him comfortable until the ambulance gets here."

She turned those brown eyes on Blazeon as she pulled off her gloves. "You! Come with me."

Chris moaned loudly.

"No, no. I can't leave him," Blazeon said, struggling back toward the exam table. Sandy, who was covering Chris with a blanket, soothed him. I tried to hold on to Blazeon and lead her from the room.

Doctor Maddie took Blazeon's arm, and together we wrestled her into the doc's office. I fell back against the wall beside the door, panting, as Doctor Maddie gently pushed Blazeon into a chair.

She sat behind her desk and sighed. "All right, Blazeon, tell me what happened."

Blazeon lifted her flowered polyester shirt and pushed it against her eyes. Doctor Maddie handed her a tissue, and she used it to blow her nose. "I heard them fighting up in the bedroom. It was over that Lynette girl. Both them boys been after that girl, and I tol' them she's no good. But do they listen? Hmph!" A heavy scowl settled on her broad chestnut features.

A short silence fell.

"Do you think he'll be okay, Doctor?" She had now changed tack and was pleading and fearful.

"Yes, I think so. So someone stabbed him while they were fighting? Who was it?"

To my surprise, Blazeon began to wail, rocking back and forth as if keening at a wake. I glanced at Doctor Maddie, and our eyes locked. For just a moment, the mother's grief fell into a very faint background as I felt myself caught completely in

Maddie's gaze. In that too-brief moment of connection, nothing else existed except one another and the energy between us. I saw her eyes widen with the same realization, and I wanted so badly to go to her. As if hearing the same silent signal, we dropped our eyes.

"Who was it, Blazeon?" she said firmly.

"Please, Doctor, don't have him arrested. It's my sister Fiercey's son. He's a good boy. A good boy. I know he didn't mean to hurt Chris, just…" She closed her eyelids, and tears cascaded along her cheeks. "He done stabbed Chris with my boy's own pocketknife his daddy gave him for Christmas."

Doctor Maddie thoughtfully steepled her fingers under her chin. She watched the woman sorrowfully. "You know I am bound to report any stabbings or shootings, Blazeon. It's the law here in Alabama. I'm sorry."

Blazeon mopped at her face again, but she sat straighter in the chair. "I know," she said. "Lord, I know."

I heard voices in the hall and slid out the door, trusting that Blazeon would stay calm. The transport ambulance had arrived, so I led them to the exam room. Soon they had Chris on a stretcher, and I tapped on the doctor's office door.

"Blazeon? They're ready. I'm assuming you want to follow them in to the hospital?"

Blazeon leapt to her feet. "Yes! Oh, Gawd. I just remembered. I left my car running out front!"

She hurried from the room, and Doctor Maddie lifted her brows in question. I shrugged.

"Are you okay, Maddie?" I asked quietly. I moved closer to her desk. "It's been a rough day."

"Yeah. Heck of a way to end the week," she said, her fingers flipping at the edge of her paper desk calendar. She looked up at me. "Are you doing all right?"

I smiled to put her at ease. "Oh, yeah. I'm just glad Chris will be okay."

She studied me a moment, her mocha eyes unreadable. "Me too. I hate that I have to report it, though. Stupid kids."

I nodded and took a deep breath. "I guess I'll go clean up exam one. Call if you need me."

Maddie said my name and, with my back to her, I closed my eyes to savor the sound. "Yes?" I said as I turned back.

"Is it okay if I pick you up at home Sunday? About eleven? We can stop for a bite on the way. It's Tropical Towers, right?"

I blinked. Oh my God. "Y—yes. That would be perfect. Apartment one ten."

A silence fell, but I felt no need to fill it. Instead, I smiled at her and left the room.

CHAPTER NINE

Maddie

The Baldwin County Elder Care facility sat on the east side of town, situated in such a way that the residents could see the ocean inlet when they relaxed on the screened-in patio. My mother sat on this patio Saturday morning, but I wasn't sure whether or not she enjoyed the view. I stood in the doorway a few minutes studying her. I never knew from one week to the next where her mood or memory would take us, so I was mentally preparing myself. It wasn't an easy task always to expect the unexpected where your mother was concerned.

Two other residents were enjoying the patio, and they stared at me curiously. I nodded and smiled at them as I approached my mother.

"*Hola, Mami, como estás?*" I said in my somewhat rusty Spanish. I didn't lean to kiss or touch her, though I wanted to. Instead, I sat across from her and rubbed my palms against my denim-clad knees. I watched her closely and saw her dim, often blank eyes brighten somewhat. She started speaking, and sadness filled me. Her Spanish had deteriorated as her Alzheimer's progressed, and I often could not understand her. I crooned to her in English, hoping she would respond in kind.

"*Mami*, are you well? Do you feel okay?"

"The food is bad, *malo*," she spat out in a heavy accent. "Why can't they move the blinds to let the sun in to warm it?"

Warm the food? I doubted it.

"Are you sure, *Mami*? Or is it sunlight for you?"

I waited a long time, but there was no answer. I started talking, telling her about my week. Our visits usually went this way. Most of her rambling these days made little sense, and instead of trying to interpret, which was frustrating at best, I would vent much as I had as a child. Back then, I would crawl into her lap in the evenings when my homework was done and tell her about the troubles of my day. She'd been sympathetic then, even empathetic, and I'd always felt whole again upon leaving her side. Those days were gone, I knew, but still…She was my *Mami*. As I talked, I moved closer and eventually took her hand in mine, caressing it with my thumb. She allowed it, which pleased me greatly. I was cautious, knowing one consequence of her illness was that her moods could shift suddenly. She could withdraw inside completely, or often she would become angry and paranoid, and those days left me painfully drained. Today was nice, holding her hand and sharing my life with her.

"She's not really any better," I told my Aunt Florida just two hours later. "But not any worse, which I guess we can be thankful for."

Aunt Florida's house was located twenty miles west of Maypearl in a little corner of the Alabama bayou. I'd stayed with her a few weeks during summers while still in school. And although I hadn't been there too many times or for any real length of time, the small pier-and-beam house that she and Uncle Thomas had shared for forty years felt like home. Especially now that Uncle Thomas and my father, his brother, had passed away and my mother had been moved out of our original home in New York.

Aunt Florida, who had gained in girth during the years since Uncle Thomas's death, lowered herself into a creaking kitchen chair and settled a glass of iced tea in front of her on the enameled table. "And you know she won't get any better, Corinthia."

I smiled out the kitchen window. No matter how many times I'd asked her to call me by my nickname, she still used my given name, saying that it was too pretty not to use. I remembered suddenly how my mother had said that name, with her particular inflection, and my gut twisted with loss.

"I know, *Tia*," I said with a sigh as I seated myself at the table. I lifted my own tea and took a deep sip. She liked it sweet, and it was a pleasant change from the unsweetened iced tea I usually drank.

"Did I tell you Esme from the church went by to visit? She told your mama a joke and even got a smile from her."

"Really?" I was impressed. "Must have been a good joke."

"Yeah, something about a turkey crossing a road to prove it wasn't chicken."

I grinned. "Oh, Lordy."

We fell silent, lost in our own thoughts. The bayou enveloped us in a warm cocoon of sound and movement. Summer frogs practiced in several barbershop quartets outside the open windows. I always understood why Florida stayed in this home, even though she was now alone and could go just about anywhere. I had married cousins in Mississippi. She could have gone there to be closer to her grandchildren. I think the mysterious inlets of the bayou country held her, and so many others, captive.

"You know," I said finally. "That's the worst part. Thinking that she might be *in* there. Just trapped somehow. Not able to respond. That's heartbreaking to me."

Florida looked at me quizzically. "And here I thought you had a medical degree," she scoffed.

"Hey, don't give me that crap. None of us know what protein folding does to the brain. All kinds of stuff could be going on up there in her brain matter."

"Hmph!" Florida raised one eyebrow and lifted her glass. "So tell me, how is that new gal working out for you?"

I choked on my own saliva and coughed until tears sprouted. "Ella? She's...she's good."

Florida laughed, a deep, rolling chuckle that swelled from inside and emerged to echo in the room. "Aw, hell, you got it sooo bad. What in the world are you going to do with yourself?"

I tried on indignance. "What do you mean?" She just stared at me, her blue eyes shining with amusement. Her head tilted to one side, and the fingers of my right hand picked at the cuticles of my left. "Yeah," I conceded. "But nothing can come of it. I told you, she works for me."

"Well, that's easy," she advised, leaning toward me. "Fire her and then date her."

"You make it sound easy," I said wistfully.

"It can be." She leaned back again.

"I have to speak at a conference over in Dothan Monday," I said.

Aunt Florida, used to rolling with my disparate changes in conversation, nodded encouragement.

I blurted the information. "Sandy usually goes with me, but she can't. So Ella's going." I lifted my eyes to hers. I was sure she could see how torn I was.

"Well, well," she muttered. "Are you gonna be okay?"

"Yes." I sighed and practiced steeling myself. "I am a professional, and I plan to act like one."

"Yep." She sighed loudly. "That old road to hell is just paved with good intentions."

CHAPTER TEN

Ella

Luckily, I'd been to a lot of conferences during various training courses, and that meant I knew how to dress—lots of layers so I could peel them off as temperatures varied. Sometimes hotels were brutally cold, and sometimes others were more like a steam bath. I knew exactly what to expect outside the hotel. That was easy: steam and more steam. I also knew that a sharp blazer over anything could dress it up to business—well, business casual, at least—and could be removed outside or if the conference rooms were warm.

I stood in front of my closet and examined the contents. It was boring, but I had a few good pieces, standards that would be acceptable. The majority of them hadn't been worn a lot, because they were mostly outfits bought for one specific occasion. I'd spent the past three years wearing some variation on hospital scrub gear or jeans and casual blouses. I hadn't dressed up much.

Sighing, I lifted my smartphone and dialed my sister. She was a fashionista and would certainly be able to help.

"It's me," I said when she answered.

"How's life treating you, El?" Her tone was always pleasant and accepting. She had been my anchor and supporter when my parents had given me grief about my life choices.

"Good, though the doc is still resisting my advances," I said in a teasing tone.

"Advances! Pish. I told you, you need to tell her how you feel. Not everybody is as clever as you are, you know. Maybe she's just obtuse and isn't picking up on any of your sly moves."

I laughed. Clever—oh, yeah. "So, guess what I'm doing tomorrow."

She chewed loudly a moment. Celery and peanut butter—it was her weakness. "Ummm, paddling the bayou again?"

"Oh, hell no. The mosquitos almost carried me off that day. The DEET kept them from biting, but oh man, they wanted me."

Jess laughed aloud. "Guess you learned a valuable lesson."

"I guess so. Between the bugs and the alligators, we just aren't supposed to be there in the backwater. It's a different world."

"You know, Brian was down there in Alabama on a job once. He was so glad to get back home to Virginia."

"Like Virginia has a lot to offer," I scoffed. I'd been to Virginia. It was green, wooded and pretty, but southwestern Virginia just didn't fit me somehow.

"Yeah, well, it's got my hubby and my two kids. Good enough for me."

"How are the kids?" Shane was fourteen now, a strapping young athlete, and his younger sister, Westie, was a shy, bookish type.

"They're good. Shane's grades are finally up again. Now, tell me what you're doing tomorrow."

"I am going to Dothan, Alabama with Doctor Maddie. Just the two of us."

A prolonged silence grew between us. "Jess?" I queried.

"The two of you. Together?" Her tone was incredulous.

"Yeah, go figure." There was too much to say, so I said very little.

"Ella, do…do you think—? I mean—"

I shook my head, even though I knew she couldn't see me. "No. It doesn't change the fact I work for her. I know her character, Jess. She'd never break ethics. Not even for love. Just my gut feeling."

"You need to leave that job, Ella. You have your MA certificate and can get a job anywhere."

I dug my fingers into my scalp. "I know. I know! I just…I don't want to be away from her now," I admitted.

I heard her sigh. "I feel for you, El. I wish there were easier answers for you."

I changed the subject. "Listen, the reason I called is I'm packing and I need your advice."

"Ahh, wanna look all dolled up for the doc," she teased. "Good idea. Make her suffer for her lofty principles."

I laughed. "Just want to look well put together, Jess. Wanna do myself proud."

"Well, you start with the basics. It's summer, so you need some linen-blend trousers—"

"Whoa! Slow down. Let's do this one item at a time." I moved back to the closet.

We spent the next forty minutes discussing outfit specifics, everything from my best color, to pairing, to alternate combinations. My sister was amazing. She had a natural affinity, via a keen interest, in the latest fashion trends. She even helped our mother and our younger sister, Barbie, choose their yearly wardrobes.

I looked at the bed, at the neatly organized clothing. It was a sedate selection, more classic than trendy, but that was what I was all about.

"Sis, you're too good to me," I said. "This looks great."

"Cool. Look, Westie's giving me the stink eye, so I'm gonna go. You can call me later if you think of any other questions."

"Oh, no. This is all good. It's only for a few days, but I'm gonna look like a million bucks."

"Well, you make sure your Doctor Maddie notices you and how good you look."

I signed off and held up a silver embedded evening shirt as I admired myself in the mirror. The dark blue set off my blond hair and deepened the blue-green of my eyes. I smiled. My Doctor Maddie. Maybe one day she really would be mine.

CHAPTER ELEVEN

Maddie

The apartment complex where Ella lived was attractive. The apartment complex I'd lived in on Cottonwood Street had been severe in comparison, and I had thought it more than adequate. Tropical Towers was lush with plants that could grow only in the temperate south. Fragrant bougainvillea in bright shades of pink, burgundy and a tinged pastel color, their white star pistils protruding impudently, ran riot everywhere here. A trio of huge magnolia trees offered a few fading blooms to greet summer, but their scent was rich and inebriating. I inhaled and held the breath in, becoming dizzy, intoxicated by the beautiful fragrance. Studying the well-placed yucca, pampas grass and perennials caused me to wonder at the grounds crew this business must employ.

I was glad Ella lived here. It suited her. She deserved such daily beauty.

I approached her ground-level apartment and opened the storm door. I found myself staring at a small stuffed rabbit, bound around the tummy with bright green ribbon and attached to the doorknocker. I smiled. The expression on the bunny's face was comical. It seemed to leer slyly at me with sideways glancing green eyes and an open, laughing mouth. There was a startling shock of white hair between the upright ears. I touched the pink triangular nose just as the door opened.

"You're here!" she said quietly.

I smiled. "Nice bunny. Yes, I'm here."

"I…I wasn't sure. Julio sometimes tells me people are here when they aren't. I think he imagines it," she said. Then she added an afterthought. "The bunny is a gift from my niece, Westie. Her name, the bunny's name, is O'Malley."

"O'Malley?" I lifted an eyebrow.

"Yes. She's Irish. Or so Westie said."

Her cheeks had pinkened, and I thought her adorable.

"Where are my manners? Come in, please," she said, gesturing me in and stepping aside.

The front room was a comfortable tableau of rescued and lovingly positioned secondhand furniture pieces. Heavy drapes were drawn most of the way across the large front window, but warm, recessed lighting made the room glow.

"I'll just be a minute," Ella said. "I promise. I know we're in a hurry."

"Not so much," I said to her retreating back. A heavy, warm body slammed against my calf. I looked down and saw a huge mass of moving black-and-gray fur. A moment later, I was staring into two large golden eyes, filled with nonchalant curiosity.

"Well, hello. You must be Julio," I said. He butted his head against my legs, and I took a seat on the sofa that was closest to me. I patted the cushion and he obediently leapt up. As a child, I had loved cats—all animals—and had always had at least one pet. I'd left my cat, Sprite, with my mom and dad when I'd left for college, and she'd died from cancer during my third year of medical school. That had been my last pet because I truly believed working the hours that I worked would not be fair to a furry child.

I lavished love on Julio. He basked in it as if it were his due as a temple cat, his loud purring filling the small room.

"So, you two look comfy," Ella said as she entered the room. She laughed, standing arms akimbo.

I had to laugh as well. "Sure is gonna be hard to leave this beautiful baby."

"Tell me about it." She came closer and perched on the sofa next to Julio. She scratched him under the chin, and he butted her chest with his head. I envied the deed. "I'm gonna miss you, baby," she crooned as she pulled him tight. He allowed the hug, and I could tell he knew his mom was leaving him. She stood and carried him to the small kitchen set off to the right. "Your food is here, and I've left Sandy a note with all the info she will need. She'll take good care of you."

Julio meowed loudly and escaped her arms to come back to me. I stood and shrugged my shoulders. "Don't blame me, Julio. The job's the job," I told him.

He mewed in response and haughtily walked away, down a long hallway that I assumed led to the bedroom.

"So, ready to go?" Ella asked, studying me.

I smiled at her. "Sure. Whenever you are."

I lifted her bag and carried it outside as she checked the apartment one final time and then securely locked the door. She looked back once as she climbed into the SUV.

"He'll be okay," I said reassuringly. "Have you ever left him before?"

She looked surprised as she buckled her seat belt. "Actually, I haven't. I got him in Virginia when I was staying with my sister and her family. We've been together ever since."

I nodded. "He has a big personality. I know he's lots of company for you." I started the car and pulled out onto Crimson Road. I headed west toward Central so I could pick up Highway 10 heading east toward Mobile.

"He really is," she replied, looking out the window as she fiddled with the handbag in her lap. "But sometimes I wonder who is the cat and who is the human."

I chuckled. "I think all cat owners have felt that way, one time or another."

"Do you have a cat? Any pets?" she asked, shifting in her seat so she could face me.

"I have in the past, many, but I don't right now. I guess I'm too...unsettled to have a pet right now."

She frowned, and I glanced at her as I turned onto Central. "What?"

"I thought Sandy told me you've been the doc here in Maypearl for like ten years or something," she said, a question evident in her tone.

"Well," I said. I paused a long beat. "I guess I have. I guess having a pet just never felt important. I work long hours sometimes, and I'm always on call, as you know."

She grinned at me, an infectious grin that I felt compelled to return. "Excuses, excuses," she said. "You just don't want to scoop a litter box."

I laughed. "Yeah, that's probably it," I agreed.

CHAPTER TWELVE

Ella

We were silent for some time, and I really didn't mind. Being with Maddie was easy. I knew I could become accustomed to it very easily. Maybe too easily. Would I let her indifference break my heart? I chewed my lip. Unrequited love was never a good idea.

"So, lunch?" Maddie said.

"Hmm?" I was drawing a blank.

She laughed and glanced at me. "Lunch? Food? How about Italian?"

"Oh." I grinned apologetically. "Yes. Yes, that sounds good."

I noted that her knuckles were white from the tense way she was gripping the steering wheel. Was she nervous? Uncomfortable? Did she dislike being with me?

She pulled off the highway near Mobile. After taking a few access roads, we ended up in front of a popular chain restaurant. I sighed, unbuckled and opened the passenger door. She sat still for a moment, as if deep in thought, and then she took in a deep breath and opened her own door. She held open the heavy glass door for me, and I preceded her inside. The mouthwatering smells of garlic and cheese washed across me, and my stomach growled in anticipation.

"Man, that smells good," Maddie muttered, right palm pressed to her abdomen.

I laughed aloud. "You read my mind."

After the hostess seated us, I lifted the menu and ran my gaze across it, even though I knew what I wanted. I was a spaghetti addict and ate it whenever the opportunity presented itself. I watched Maddie as she studied the menu, and then dropped my gaze. She was such a fine, beautiful woman. How could I even dare to hope that she would be interested in me?

"So, it's great to finally have this time to get to know one another a little better," she said, setting her menu aside and leaning her forearms on the table.

I cleared my throat. "Yes, it is. We stay so busy, usually." I hesitated. "I have to confess, I had a preconceived image of what small-town doctoring was like. I figured there was a lot of sitting around, waiting for something to happen."

Maddie laughed. I was happy to see that she wasn't offended by my stereotyping. "Yeah, I think I might have thought that once upon a time, as well," she said, running one palm across her forehead. She used both hands to smooth her dark hair, and I realized suddenly that there was some curl to it. She wore it up, usually, so I hadn't noticed before.

She eyed me quizzically. I must have been staring. I lowered my eyes and was about to speak again, but the server arrived.

"Good afternoon, ladies," she said cheerily. "What can I get you two to drink today?"

She was young and self-confident, as evidenced by the bright orange streak dyed into her dark hair. She had a band of freckles across her nose and cheeks and an engaging smile, the teeth covered in neon orange braces. She waited, smiling, pad and pen perched in her fingers.

"Tea," I said. "Iced tea, no sugar."

"Lemon?" she asked.

"Sure, that's fine."

"And you, ma'am?" She turned her attention to Maddie, who was staring at me. She stirred herself and ordered unsweetened iced tea, as well.

"Okay, have a look at the menu, and I'll be right back." She scurried off, her step bouncy.

I looked at Maddie, and she looked at me. "Everything okay?" I asked nervously.

She waved one hand and let loose a mild raspberry through her full lips. Her eyes were amused. "It's easy to forget what real life is like, that's all," she said, shrugging. "Do you know, I have been in school for more than a decade? Hell, almost fifteen years, if you count apprenticeship."

"You worked under the previous doc, Sandy said."

She nodded. "I did. His name was Richard. Doctor Richard Pembroke."

"What was he like?" I rested my chin in one upraised palm, my elbow on the table. I so enjoyed watching her talk. I liked the way her lean, squarish jaw moved. I longed to touch her face.

"Oh, a nice guy. Big partier. I think that's really why he never married. He was having just too much fun playing with the local widows." She grinned sheepishly.

I laughed. "So a ladies' man, huh? And you? I mean…" I blushed and hoped she wouldn't notice. "Not a ladies' man, I know, but you're not married, I understand?"

I glanced at her and saw that her eyes were fairly dancing with merriment. "*Me gusta la forma sonrojar,*" she said, her tongue effortlessly rolling out the words.

I gasped. I had no idea what she'd said, but I could feel the words push against my groin and up through my midsection. The way her lips and tongue had moved—

"Oh, I'm sorry," she said, obviously sensing some reaction from me. "I just said I like it when you blush. I don't usually speak Spanish anymore. That was rude."

I hastened to reassure her. "No, it's fine. You speak Spanish beautifully."

She smiled. "It's sort of my native language."

"Oh, right." *Duh*, I told myself. "You don't have much of an accent and I forget."

She unfolded her napkin and placed it in her lap. "I have forgotten a lot of it. I've spent almost as much time in the states as in the Caribbean when I was growing up. Texas too. And no, I'm not."

"Not?" She'd lost me.

"Married."

The server brought our drinks and took our orders. I was oddly unsurprised when we both ordered salads with oil and vinegar on the side and spaghetti with marinara sauce.

"You're not married either," she said, straightening her knife and fork.

"Nope. And probably never will be."

"Why do you say that?"

I studied her, wondering how much to trust her. She was, after all, my employer, and we had never discussed anything like this before. "Let's just say I'm not a fan of traditional marriage roles."

She watched me in silence for a long beat. I saw her open her mouth to speak, but the server brought our salads. She fell silent and thoughtful as she dressed her salad. I did the same, also in silence.

"There are untraditional marriages," she said finally.

"Ah, so, you're...you're a supporter of gay marriage?"

She raised her eyebrows. "Of course! Of any LGBTQ marriage."

Just hearing this made warm joy course through me. "Oh, I'm glad," I said. "I feel the same way."

"So you would get married, then?"

Was she outing me? I couldn't lie to her, so I tried to be noncommittal. "Yes. Yes, I would," I said, and then I bent my head industriously over my salad. I could sense that she had as well, and silence reigned for a few moments.

"Going back to what you said earlier, it is amazing how many patients we see." She leaned to sip her tea. "And that's not factoring in an aging population, because we are a family practice and see all ages."

I nodded in agreement. "I guess being the only real doctor in the whole town of more than a thousand people makes you in demand."

"But people don't stay sick, you know? You'd think the majority would be well most of the time," she said, spearing a cube of cucumber with her fork.

I placed my fork beside my plate and dabbed my mouth with my napkin. "I guess that it has to be frustrating for you."

"How so?" She watched me expectantly.

"Most of what we see is chronic carelessness." I waved a hand dismissively before she could object with political correctness. "I don't mean that in a judgmental way. It's just America. It's what we do. We eat the wrong foods, too much of the wrong foods. Fast food, pizza, sodas. It's become our common diet, and it leads to high blood pressure, fatty liver, diabetes one and two and heart disease. These conditions have to be managed, and that falls on you."

She nodded thoughtfully as she chewed. "This is true. And I can't say to them 'eat this, eat that.' They don't hear me, and even if they did, what choices are out there?"

"And then there's plastics everywhere, on the land, in our water, our food. Every product we buy could cause cancer or immunity or conception issues." I knew that Blazeon Hughes had been trying for a handful of years to get pregnant, but out-of-office confidentiality issues prevented me from mentioning her now, even with her doctor.

"I sometimes, you know, think of the future and what it will be like. It's not a good picture in my mind. I want to fix it, but it is…beyond what I can do. This is why I travel and do these talks. It's so issues can be out there and maybe dealt with. It's what little I can do."

I studied her as she spoke. Her accent became more pronounced the longer she talked, and I was enchanted by it and by her.

"Here you go, ladies. Nice hot spaghetti. There's fresh grated parmesan in that shaker by the salt and pepper," our server said as she placed a large flat bowl in front of each of us and then a fragrant basket of bread on the table between us. "Enjoy! Let me know if you need anything else."

"Fresh, hot bread," I breathed in a low whisper when the server had left us. Maddie caught my eye, and we both laughed as we reached for the bread at the same time. We ended up splitting a small loaf of white bread with rosemary baked into it.

I slathered mine with butter as Maddie took a hefty bite of her buttered half and groaned with pleasure. I felt the groan viscerally, and I was sure my face was blushing as I bit into mine. "Oh man, this is good," I said.

Maddie nodded. "Ah, America," she said.

CHAPTER THIRTEEN

Maddie

Spending this travel time with Ella had finally put me at ease about being with her. How could it not? She was a joy to talk with, and I found myself throwing my own reticence to the wind. I felt as though I could trust her with the me that I usually kept hidden away. I felt no judgment from her, only acceptance of me as a woman.

As a physician, we find early on that we have to hold our emotion and our true self in check. Patients could be amazing manipulators, and I had encountered my fair share while interning in Texas. We had to remain aloof and maybe even be a bit intimidating. Drug and emotional addicts were what we cut our doctoring teeth on, and you learned to ferret these folks out right away. And to never encourage them in these practices. We were the saviors of health, not enablers. Ella seemed to understand this and wasn't so in awe of me as a physician. She saw the person underneath, and I was grateful for that.

My one worry was that I would inadvertently lead her on, encouraging a relationship that really could never be. This was my only reservation about spending time with her. I frowned as I drove. That and the fact being so close to her made my blood pound under my skin.

After lunch, we drove the next three hours in a nonstop chatter exchange. I learned about her two sisters and her niece and nephew, even down to their favorite colors. Her parents, though, were a different matter indeed.

"But don't you ever see them?" I asked, thinking of how I'd give anything to have both my parents close again. I glanced at her to find her lips set in a grim line.

"No. They have made it clear that they want no part of my life. They live in New Mexico, so I'm as far from them as I can be. We both like it that way."

"So you left there, when? After high school?" I gave a signal and shifted into the right lane so I could slow my speed.

"No, after college. I worked my way through CNM for my basics, then my physician assistant studies through UNM. I moved away right after and went to my sister's place in Virginia." She fell into a thoughtful silence. "I liked it there, and my sister's family was great, really welcoming. But...well, there was just nothing for me there."

"So, how did you get to Alabama?" I was curious about her life and the problem with her parents.

"It was the ad you listed in the APPA journal. I saw it in Virginia and thought that Maypearl, Alabama seemed like a nice little town."

"Oh, that's right!" I mentally thanked Sandy for the listing and then grunted and called Ella on this. "You were running away, weren't you? Trying to strike out on your own."

She shrugged. "I guess."

"What is it with your parents?" I asked finally.

She didn't say anything for a long beat, and I thought maybe she wouldn't answer.

"Let's just say we have a fundamental difference in values and lifestyle," she said sullenly.

"Ahh, conservatives!" I offered. "They don't like the fact that you're...vegetarian! Yes, that's it. The carnivores! How dare they?"

Luckily, she got my humor and laughed along with me, effectively dispelling the gloom from before.

"So, why are you in Alabama?" she asked.

I told her about meeting Richard while I was still in school and about how he had invited me into his practice.

"Wow, talk about being in the right place at the right time," she exclaimed.

"I guess so." I shrugged. "My father passed back in ninety-nine and my mother started developing dementia at right about the same time. She's been on preventative medications since, and though we managed to slow progression, she's had to move into a full care facility. When I accepted Richard's offer, I moved her down here a few months later. She's over at Baldwin County Elder Care."

"That's a beautiful place."

"Yes, and she seems happy there. I go see her every Saturday, unless I have an emergency on call." I didn't go into detail about her now-vacant eyes and about how much I missed the person she had been.

"That's good that you brought her here. Anything could have happened to her in New York with no one to look out for her," Ella said, leaning to turn down the air conditioning fan on her side.

I nodded. "I have an aunt here in Alabama too. My father's brother's wife. Uncle Thomas passed, as well, so we are sort of all that's left, though she has three kids and a pile of grandchildren scattered over in Mississippi. She goes to see my mother some, too."

Ella studied me. "Are you close?"

I sighed. "As close as I can be to anyone, I guess. Oh, wait, that sounded pitiful. I mean with my job. It's demanding." I backpedaled desperately as Ella laughed.

"I guess that's true," Ella said wistfully. I found myself wondering what she was thinking. "It must be hard to have any life when you are the only doctor in a whole town."

I nodded thoughtfully. "True. Though to be honest..."

She turned to me. "Though to be honest, what?"

I know my face was flushed. "Um, well. I think you might not be the only one running from something."

She fell silent. After a long beat, I looked over and saw that she was smiling to herself. I was seriously confused.

I spied the exit to the hotel and we soon entered a wide drive bordered by huge mounds of green, tropical foliage on either side. The big chain hotel had been engaged by the Furth College Medical Assistant Training Center for The Southeastern Society for Family Physicians' annual conference.

A cadre of my contemporaries greeted us raucously as soon as we entered the lobby. The SSFP, made up of more than two hundred sixty family physicians working in the lower southeastern states, was responsible for setting policy and providing support for practitioners in my field. I'd been a member since Richard had introduced them to me nine years ago. They provided a good, informative newsletter, filled with fascinating case studies and innovative advances in the discipline of family medicine.

I guessed the reason I liked family medicine so much was the sheer amount of variety I encountered. Most other specialties saw the same issues day after day. Family practitioners were able to deal with the full gamut of medicine, from infants to geriatric patients. Not that the work we did wasn't repetitive and predictable. It was. An upper respiratory infection was an upper respiratory infection. Except when it was pneumonia, bronchitis or even an aspect of pulmonary hypertension. We had to ferret out that information. I'd worked with some horribly jaded family physicians, true, but when you met one who was still excited by a challenge, it was special and rewarding.

"A lot of people are still looking at you," Ella said at my elbow. We had just checked in and had relinquished our bags to the bellhop.

I smiled at her. "Nope, looking at you. They are used to Sandy, so I know they are all wondering who you are."

"Oh, great," she muttered.

"Don't worry. I'll introduce you to everyone. You can skirt all the interrogative questions if you want to. I won't mind."

"So, if I'm a complete rude boor, it won't reflect badly on you?" she responded teasingly.

I was enchanted by her sparkly, smiling eyes. How could one person be so...cute?

I could only shake my head, overwhelmed by my attraction to her.

"Maddie! How are you?" Oscar hailed me as he approached. "How was the drive over?"

I shook his outstretched hand. "It was good, went quickly. Ella, allow me to introduce you to Dr Oscar Quillen. He has a practice outside Jackson, Mississippi. Oscar, Ella Lewis, my new medical assistant."

"Ahh, is Sandy well?" he asked, mild alarm etched on his features.

Ella stepped forward and offered her hand. "Oh yes, she's fine. It was just a family commitment that she didn't want to miss. Hopefully, I'll be able to walk in her big old shoes, at least temporarily."

Quillen was as enchanted by Ella as I was. After studying her with admiring eyes, he smiled and graciously took her hand, bending to press his lips to the back of it. "Miss Lewis. It's delightful to meet you," he said.

I saw Mrs. Quillen approaching so jumped in quickly. "Ella, this is Priscilla, Dr Quillen's lovely wife."

Priscilla, a very attractive middle-aged woman, pressed one palm to Oscar's back as she extended her hand to Ella. "Very nice to meet you, Ella. From where do you know our dear Maddie?"

She smiled at Ella, and I could see the gears in her mind whirring, wondering if there was a new scandal brewing.

"Ella is our newest medical assistant at the office. She's been with us about six months now, I think." I looked to Ella for confirmation.

"Yes. I, luckily, answered an ad, and I'm very glad to be part of Doctor Maddie's team," Ella offered.

"We hear great things about Maddie's practice. Don't we, Oscar?" She looked to her husband.

Oscar nodded. "Yes, that piece she published on geriatric medication management was an eye-opener." Oscar and Priscilla were both beaming at me like proud parents, making me decidedly uncomfortable.

"Hmm, I haven't read that one yet," Ella interjected. "Can you tell me what it was about?"

Effectively, thankfully, diverting them from me, she looped an arm in each of their elbows and walked them leisurely to one side.

I admired her technique with a broad smile as I took a seat in the lobby and checked my phone for messages.

CHAPTER FOURTEEN

Ella

The hotel was spectacular. Located on a small man-crafted lake made from Cypress Creek, it fronted onto a large, resort-like landscape. It was actually far grander than anything I had seen in my thirty-two years. Well, American grand. Europe certainly offered more, but in a more compact package.

The Quillens had abandoned me finally. As Maddie was talking with a group of her peers, I had snuck away to wander the hotel by myself.

My first stop had been through huge glass doors and onto what was called—according to a mounted plaque—the Grand Terrace. The heat was palpable, even though the terrace was fully roofed and the ceiling peppered with slowly gyrating ceiling fans. They did amazingly little to dispel the heat. Even so, the terrace was well populated with tourists and apparently a number of those who were attending this medical conference.

The program I had filched from the concierge desk stated that Maddie's presentation would be at ten the next morning. This would give us time for a leisurely breakfast. I hoped, anyway. I wasn't sure what her preparatory procedures were and made a mental note to ask her at dinner.

"Hello."

I turned and saw a classically beautiful woman. She was about my height, but slimmer, with long, frothing blond hair. Her eyes were crystal blue, and they regarded me with an amused expression laced with attraction. I looked at her full pink lips and felt my mouth go dry.

"Hello back," I managed to choke out.

"Are you here for business or pleasure?"

The way she drawled the word *pleasure* intrigued me. My gaydar buzzed, and I wondered if she was really coming on to me.

"Umm, business, I guess. I'm here with my boss. For the family practice medical conference. How about you?"

She sighed and rolled her eyes. "My dad. He's an admin over at Furth. I work for him part-time, and he insisted I be here. You know…to press the flesh."

There was that inflection again. My heart started to race just a bit and I wondered if it was from fear or from attraction to this beautiful and certainly accommodating woman. "An administrator's bailiwick," I responded quietly.

"Exactly. How about you and I have a little iced tea and you can tell me all about yourself?" She tilted her head expectantly.

I was torn. I could feel Maddie, who I so wanted to fall in love with, in the hotel, oh-so close, but here was this warm and willing beauty. I looked deeply into her eyes and saw a social vulnerability lurking behind her bravado. It was an emotion I understood completely. I'd been there.

"Sure," I said, nodding. "I'd love a glass of tea. What's your name?"

She laughed and shook her head as she extended her hand. "Dixie Odelia."

I grinned as I took her hand. "Ella Lewis."

We moved to a nearby table that was laden with stacked stemware and several large glass dispensers of tea and lemonade. We chatted about the beautiful hotel as we prepared our beverages and then moved to a small table and seated ourselves.

"So, Dixie, have you always lived in Alabama?" I asked as we settled on the round metal chairs.

"Oh, Lordy no. I was born and brought up in Saint Mary Parish over in Louisiana, down on the Atchafalaya Bay. They tell me my daddy worked in a grocery store there until he decided to go to college. And look at him today," she said with a dimpled smile.

"Is it hard being his kid and also working for him?"

She nodded. "It is. He's a demanding fella, all the way around. I think, because he didn't come from much, he's always worried that he's gonna topple off that pedestal he's managed to climb up on." She leaned forward. "Having a daughter like me...you know...hasn't helped much."

"Yeah, my parents just don't get it either."

"And get this, my brother's gay. Big time." She sat back and grinned like the cat that got the canary.

I laughed aloud. "Oh, no, poor Dad."

She nodded grandly. "Yeah, and he's like, always in trouble. Gay drama this, gay drama that. At least I am a bit more genteel about it."

I studied her. "So, are you in a relationship right now?"

Her gaze lifted to mine, and she winked. "Not yet, sugar. Shall we give it a shot?"

Whoa. My pounding heart was definitely from fear this time. "Well, I'm sort of...involved." I thought of Maddie's soft brown eyes and about how very much I wanted them to look at me with love. Was I dreaming about what she and I could become? I looked at Dixie's sweet face and faltered. Suppose Maddie never fell in love with me? Was I to be alone forever, waiting? "Well, maybe—" I started to speak but was interrupted.

"There you are!" Maddie said as she approached. Her eyes flicked to Dixie. "Well, I had no idea you knew Ms. Odelia," she added quietly.

I noted her sudden tenseness and wondered at it. "Oh no, we just met," I said, smiling at Dixie. "We thought we'd try to cool off. This heat is brutal."

"Yes, it is," Maddie muttered.

"Dr Salas, it's very good to see you again," Dixie said, her voice like a purr. "Won't you come join us for a little iced tea?"

Maddie cleared her throat and looked decidedly uncomfortable. "Thank you for the offer, but your father sent us to our rooms to have a little rest before dinner. It was a long drive from Maypearl and I thought we should take advantage of that bit of downtime."

"Well, pooh," she replied. Her face brightened. "I guess I'll just go up as well." She stood and pulled me up, linking an arm in mine as she led the way into the hotel. Maddie filed along behind us, and I could feel her scowl. I didn't need to see it.

We stepped into one of the luxurious mirrored elevators, and Maddie pressed a button.

"Omigosh! I see y'all are on six. I am too," Dixie said brightly. "We should all get together and have a girls' night."

I saw Maddie's discomfort and jumped in quickly. "That's a great idea, but not tonight. The doc has a presentation in the morning, so it's gonna be an early night."

She actually pouted, shoving out her bottom lip. "But what about you, sugar? Surely you can have a little fun."

I opened my mouth to speak but didn't have the chance.

"She has to help me prepare," Maddie said tersely. "This is a working trip, not a vacation."

Dixie made a face and rolled her eyes behind Maddie's back.

"Maybe some other time," I said politely.

The elevator opened, and I followed Maddie rapidly along the hallway. Dixie veered off with a small wave.

CHAPTER FIFTEEN

Maddie

"Dinner is at seven but the mixer is at six thirty. Shall we meet here and go down together?" I couldn't bring myself to look at her—for so many reasons.

"That sounds good," Ella replied. "I think I'll go stretch out for a minute." She turned away but turned back quickly. "You should too, Maddie. Dinner could run long."

I nodded and stepped into my room. I held the door partially cracked until I heard her enter her room and shut the door.

Wearily, I slumped onto the bed. I was quickly coming to loathe these gatherings. Pretentious people acting especially pretentious. I wondered again why I even bothered attending. It was probably some publish-or-perish baggage lingering from my time in school. That and the team mentality of my medical training. I chided myself. I didn't need that crap anymore. I kicked off my shoes, slid out of my blazer and draped it across a nearby chair.

During the past few months, I had been a voyeur, watching my discontent grow exponentially. I had agonized about it, wondering if the career path I'd chosen was no longer sustaining and challenging me. I had finally ruled that idea out. I was still obsessed by medicine. Indeed, if I had to name the one redeeming feature that salved my discontent, it would *be* medicine. Though I had no ready answers to explain my angst, I did know that seeing Ella with another woman had lit a strange fire under me that was exhausting and infuriating. I did not like it. Not one bit.

Acknowledging this fact caused me to realize that, just as the letter B followed the letter A, my feelings for Ella were at the root of my discontent. Longing for her passively just wasn't going to be enough anymore. At any time, she could slip into another's arms. And that might very well be my undoing.

I rose and walked to the floor-to-ceiling windows that looked out over a small lake, the center fountain spraying water that misted into a rainbow in the late-afternoon sunlight. Men and women, in various stages of undress, mingled on the bright concrete below, and the business part of the town of Dothan stretched to the horizon.

Though I tried to tell myself that it didn't matter, that I was too busy, too career focused, too worried about local gossip, deep in my heart I knew that I could not let her go. I could not let another have her.

Clasping my hands together, I shuddered. For years, I had been uninvolved, in life and in love. The job was everything to me. After all, I had few familial distractions, a nonexistent social life and my busy mind craved educational stimulus. I had used all of that as a crutch to deny myself what I really wanted. Who I really wanted. Doing so was so much easier than trying to commit and perhaps being hurt again. No, fooled. That was what Amanda had done to me when I had been a busy resident. She had fooled me into believing that she cared when she really hadn't.

I moved restlessly back to the bed and stretched out on my back. I was coming up on my fortieth year. Could I risk that again? Could I risk throwing myself wholeheartedly into a relationship? It had been so long now. Would I be able to be a good partner? Was I too set in my ways to be accommodating to another person? Then there was the issue of coming out in a small town. Oh, I knew the residents there talked about weird, single Doctor Maddie. Lord only knew what they surmised about my bachelorette status. I'd place bets there weren't many who thought it was because I was attracted to women instead of men. There were lots of local men, widowers or twenty-somethings, who would love a little private doctor time, but lesbians in Maypearl were few and far between. And actually, I was grateful for that. It was a good excuse.

I rolled onto my stomach, cupping my chin in my folded hands in lieu of a pillow. God, I wanted Ella. I wanted to hold her body close, tuck my face into her neck, kiss the dimple that often appeared in her left cheek. I wanted to spend more time getting to know her, to learn all her quirks, her daily habits. I knew then, with horrible, beautiful clarity, that I had to have her in my life. Even if it meant changing all the comfortable honeycombs I had built in my life. Was I ready? I didn't know. But I was willing to try.

She was breathtaking when I met her outside our rooms that evening. She had on a sleeveless black one-piece jumpsuit with a lovely low neckline. It was mostly form fitting with a little give, and over this, she had a lightweight black-and-white tunic-type jacket with a handkerchief hem. Her shoes were black, strappy flat sandals. I thought she had showered as well, as had I, because she smelled soapy and fresh underneath her usual perfume. She smiled shyly at me, and my earlier bad mood vanished as I looked into her beautiful emerald eyes.

I moved close and offered my arm. She nodded and took it.

"You look beautiful," I said quietly.

"Why, thank you. You look pretty nice yourself," she responded with a soft laugh.

I looked down at my navy blazer, dark jeans and white button-down shirt. "Well, everything's clean, at least," I said, which set her off into a spate of giggles.

"Should I be nervous?" she asked as we entered the elevator.

I studied her, wondering at her fear as I selected the lobby level button. She was always so good with people. "No. Doctors are people just like anyone else. They may be more jaded, but don't let that throw you. Just be your usual charming self." I looked away from her so she wouldn't see the emotion I was sure was reflected on my face.

Surprising me, Ella took my hand and interlaced her fingers with mine. "Thanks, Doc," she whispered.

We rode the rest of the way in silence. She let my hand go as the doors opened, and we stepped into a mass of conference attendees who were crowded at the lobby bar having predinner drinks. My hand tingled pleasurably for a very long time.

CHAPTER SIXTEEN

Ella

Dinner was in one of the huge ballrooms off the north end of the main floor, and I was glad to see it. Several drinks on an empty stomach weren't doing old Ella any favors. We'd spent the past hour working the crowd of more than two hundred physicians and their wives or husbands that filled the bar just off the lobby. I was talked out, and I knew without a doubt that I would remember none of their names. They were a mass of exhausted faces and smiling mouths filled with perfect teeth.

"You sighed," Maddie said, coming closer. "Is anything wrong?"

"Nope. It just seems…late."

"Shoot. The party is just getting started, honey child," Maddie responded, humor lightening her voice.

I turned in surprise. It wasn't like Maddie to…have fun. I smiled at her, happy to see her loosening up and relaxing. "How much have you had to drink?" I asked.

She looked at me, brown eyes dancing merrily. "I matched you drink for drink, my dear."

"Uh-oh. We're in trouble, then," I joked.

"Yep. And I'd like to add that I can drink you under the table any day," she responded.

I nodded. I wasn't going to argue that point.

"Well, there you two are," Dixie exclaimed as she approached us. "I totally missed y'all at the mixer."

That hadn't been an accident on my part, but politeness garnered a response. "I can't begin to tell you how many people we spoke to. There's just not enough hours in the day," I said, waving my hand helplessly.

I could feel Maddie tensing next to me, and I wondered again at the animosity she harbored toward Dixie.

"Actually, my daddy sent me over. He wants y'all to sit at our table. Come on with me, and we'll get you settled." She turned and looked back over her shoulder expectantly. I couldn't help but notice how her floral dress hugged her hips and flared out over her outer thighs.

As we followed her, Maddie surprised me yet again by taking my upper arm in her warm hand and pulling our bodies close together as we made our way to the table. Once there, Dixie indicated a chair to my left. "You can sit here next to me, Ella. We can catch up on our girl talk."

Maddie took the chair to my right, and we seated ourselves as all the tables filled around us.

I had met Wilson Odelia, Senior Director of Education Operations at Furth College, at the mixer. He was a tall, gawky man, reminding me much of the actor Jimmy Stewart. His voice was soft and heavily laden with a Southern drawl. I had enjoyed listening to him. He sat on the other side of Dixie, and I was relieved. Perhaps his presence would tone down her overt advances to me. They made me uncomfortable and completely confused me. If I'd never met Maddie, I might have enjoyed it. Now, my dealings with Dixie made me feel as though I trod on uneven ground.

Dixie's mother was seated at the table, as well. Her name was Annagrace Price Odelia, and that was exactly how she had introduced herself. She was a battened-down Southern Belle, bristling over with fake good cheer and politeness. The rest of the handful of diners at our table I'd met in passing, and I smiled and nodded in greeting. Maddie seemed to know the young man to her right very well, and they immediately began talking earnestly about cardiac medications.

"Did you have a good rest?" Dixie asked. The server approached with a pitcher of tea. At our nods, he filled our glasses.

"I did. I took a nice long, hot shower and looked over the town information. Dothan is a nice city, larger than I expected. There's a lot to do here."

She nodded and shifted so she was facing me. "Maybe sometime when you're not working, you'd want to come back. You can stay at my place. I have a little bungalow over on Mimosa. I can show you all around. We have one good bar, if you know what I mean, and they do country dancing. It's fun."

I studied my hands. Was that something I wanted to do? At one point in my life, I would have said absolutely. I longed for those days again but would not trade my new feelings toward Maddie for them. Now, I needed to dodge the invitation politely. "That would be nice. I will certainly give it some thought. Thank you for the offer."

She pursed her lips and shrugged. "A gal's gotta try," she said. "The offer stands, though," she added with a deep sigh.

A server brought salad and bread, distracting her briefly.

"You know, I'm going through a bit of a strange time, right now," I said, in an effort to explain.

She shrugged again. "It's okay. Plenty of time." She took up a forkful of salad.

I felt someone watching me and turned to find that it was Maddie. "Tom was just telling me that heart disease is caused as much by not eating the right vegetable fats as eating the wrong ones." She was studying me to see how I would respond. Was she testing my intelligence? An odd concept, but I felt I was up to the challenge.

I nodded. "I read a study that said the essential fatty acids we need are best acquired from nuts and plant oils. People think a low-fat diet, or no-fat diet, for that matter, will help them prevent heart disease—"

"When actually they are hurting their health," she finished for me.

"Exactly."

We fell silent as we enjoyed our first course. People conversed all around us, but I couldn't, or perhaps wouldn't, follow their conversations. I was feeling Maddie's energy. At work, we had very little contact and even less closeness for prolonged periods of time. I found myself sensing her with every part of my being and thoroughly relishing it. I toyed with my salad, unwilling to eat and move on to a new sense sensation.

"Ella."

I turned to Maddie. "Yes?"

"Are you happy working with us?"

Why was she asking me that? "You're not firing me, are you?"

She sighed and folded her hands together on the table. "No. I have no reason to do that. You're a good fit. Sandy sings your praises all the time."

"And you feel the same?"

Her brown eyes lifted to me, and I saw wonderful things there. Things that made my toes curl and new hope kindle in my heart. Maybe she did see me. Maybe she did have feelings for me. "I am very glad you are there, Ella. Very glad."

CHAPTER SEVENTEEN

Maddie

Dinner was over at last. I'd been distracted and certainly a worse conversationalist than usual. Feeling Ella at my side kept pulling me into erotic imaginings. It was very hard to talk shop with my contemporaries when all I could think about was ravishing the beautiful, enchanting woman next to me. It was like some confining gate had been opened earlier when I was in my room. I had realized that I could no longer deny the chemistry between us. Now, that chemistry was taking me over.

The dinner had one advantage, however, because Dixie had been unable to spend too much quality time with my Ella, even though they were seated next to one another. Dixie's father had demanded Dixie's time. Tom Weathers, next to me, had monopolized a lot of my time talking about new research as Ella sat quietly, as if lost in her own thoughts.

"So, what would you like to do now?" I asked Ella as we rose to leave the dining room.

"Hmm. Do you need to be somewhere?"

"No, not really. I see these people every year, and not much changes."

She studied me with an intense blue-green gaze. "They bore you, don't they?" she whispered.

Wilson Odelia approached, Dixie at his heels. His wife stood behind them to one side, speaking desultorily with another Southern matron. "So, Maddie, you're settled in, then? We have you scheduled for ten, then Quillen will go next and Anderson after lunch. It's stacked up to be quite a program. We're excited."

I could see how excited he really was by the dull cast in his eyes.

"That sounds good, Wilson. Is the room on the program?"

"It is. You'll be speaking in suite one hundred two. We expect a good-sized turnout."

I smiled. "I hope not too many, or my shyness might kick in."

Wilson waved a hand, brushing my words aside. "Never known you to choke up yet," he said. "Once you start talking about something you're passionate about, I think the rest of us just plumb disappear."

I laughed and winked at Ella. "That's true. Medicine does seem to be a consuming passion of mine."

Wilson shook his head as Dixie studied me, eyes narrowed. "I wish I enjoyed my passion as much as you. Dealing with student issues has absolutely lost all its charm," he admitted.

I laid a palm on his shoulder for a moment, in camaraderie. "Sometimes it becomes real hard to see the wheat beyond the chaff," I told him. I knew a bit of his story from previous discussions, and I felt badly that his career wasn't living up to his dreams. Especially when he had worked so very hard to get where he was.

"Now, Daddy," Dixie said nervously, clasping his arm. "You know you don't mean that. Why, just last week you were raving about the Camellia Society and the money they raised for the blood drive bus."

Wilson patted her hand. "Yes, Dixie, they're good kids, I know. I just get tired sometimes, and tomorrow's gonna be a very busy, hectic day." He turned and extended his hand. "Ella, it's been a real pleasure getting to know you, my dear. I'm sure Maddie will treat you right."

Ella took the hand and enclosed it in both of hers. "I believe she will continue to do so, sir. And I'll be sure and wave at you in passing tomorrow as you race by."

They both laughed, and Dixie smiled widely, dimpling her cheek. "I told you she was just the sweetest thing, didn't I, Daddy?"

"Truer words were never spoken, dear Dixie. Now, let's go see what your mama is up to."

They wandered off toward Annagrace, and I could see the relief on her pinched face. I glanced toward Ella. I couldn't imagine her being so peeved at me, but then, how well did I know her, really? I needed to remedy that.

"Hey, Ella. Want to go have another drink and visit a while?"

She smiled and tilted her head to one side. "Absolutely. It feels good to break routine, doesn't it?"

I nodded. "Yeah, it's a big step for me, but this year, I feel like I have a very good reason to do everything differently."

I could see her mulling this and prayed that she would understand my meaning and come to the right realization. I wanted her to know how I felt about her, but how could I say the words when I wasn't sure I knew them anymore?

"I think there's a lounge on the fourth floor. What say we check it out?" I suggested.

"That's a lovely idea, Maddie. Let's go."

We piled onto the elevator with acquaintances and strangers, making polite conversation with them until we got off on the fourth floor.

The lounge was small, very cozy, with dim lighting and soft music playing. Several tables were filled with loudly conversing people, but I spied a back corner that was almost deserted. "Let's go back there," I told her, pointing to the table.

Once we were seated and our drinks ordered, I just sat a moment enjoying her beauty. Slanting light fell across her face, making her eyes glisten as they moved.

"Ella, I...I want to get to know all about you. Everything about you."

She grinned. "Everything? That's a tall order."

"Maybe. Maybe, but aren't..." I paused and leaned forward, my forearms on the table. "Maybe we're meant to connect with one another."

She raised her eyebrows. "You mean us, or people in general?"

I squirmed in frustration. I wasn't good at this dance of seduction. "Well, all people, obviously, but I meant us, you and me, right now." I waited anxiously for her response.

"I'd like that. For you to know everything about me. And I want to know you the same way," she said, her cheek dimpling in a deep smile.

Our drinks arrived, and I took a large gulp of scotch to fortify myself. "Okay, I'll start. I'm not very good at sharing. You know, I...well, I seem to be more comfortable with books than people, I guess." I dropped my eyes, embarrassed by the confession.

"I do okay with people, as I think my life has been very different from yours, but I have to admit that I have a real jones for reading. I read every single evening. Actually, any chance I get."

That was interesting. "Fiction or nonfiction?" I asked.

She chuckled. "Both. I'm a sucker for the written word. My sister Jess says I will read cereal boxes."

I laughed. How many times had my father said that to me? "I'm the same way. I read a lot of medical journals, but I just love a medical thriller. Have you heard of Robin Cook? He's a retired doctor from Harvard who writes—"

"Oh gosh, yes!" she exclaimed. "Which is your favorite? I loved...Well, did you read *Fever*? It's one of his older ones, but I thought he did a great job with that one. I thought the girl with leukemia seemed a little unrealistic, but the tension in the families is very well done."

I had to laugh. What were the chances that Ella would be a Cook fan? "Yes, loved that one. I think I've read them all. I just picked up *Death Benefit* but haven't read it yet. I hear it's good. I want to read that one before I read *Nano*. It's like a series. Have you read them?"

Ella was studying me, her eyes very tender. Fear quaked through me. Would she be the one? Would she be the one who would understand my weirdness and accept it? Even love it? Could she love and appreciate the real me? Could she understand that a good book was comfortable for me, much more so than traveling the minefield of personal relationships?

"I haven't read those two yet though I have them at home," she whispered, gaze filled with wonder. "You'll have to read them first and tell me how you liked them."

I dropped my gaze, embarrassed. "I will." Her words spoke of a future, and I reveled in that.

CHAPTER EIGHTEEN

Ella

"Do you have brothers and sisters, Maddie? I just realized I haven't asked you that."

It was late, almost midnight, but I couldn't break the solid connection we had forged during the evening. We had so much in common; it was like we'd been crafted for one another. We were a perfect pairing, and I was so very sad that we hadn't met before. So many years had been wasted with others and alone.

She twirled the rocks glass in front of her. She was nursing the last finger of amber scotch, and I wondered if she was as loath to break our connection as I was. How could we say goodnight now? I was so filled with her, as I hoped she was with me. "No. I'm an only child. My mother was RH negative."

I nodded. "Glad you are here, then."

Her glowing eyes bored into mine. "Me too."

I felt an erotic thrill race through me. I so wanted to take her upstairs, to my bed, so I could know her body as well as I now knew her mind. I sighed shakily. No, that would have to wait. The time wasn't right.

But will it ever be right when you get back home?, whispered the devil on my left shoulder. I knew that this place and this time was rarified, not the norm for either of us.

"We need to go to bed," I said without thinking. At Maddie's raised eyebrow, I blushed crimson and backpedaled. "You have a presentation in the morning, I mean. You need to rest. I'm supposed to be looking after you, Sandy said."

She sighed and gulped her drink. "You're right. I've…I've really enjoyed getting to know you, Ella."

I smiled at her. "It's been a perfect night, Maddie, but I'm sure you had work to do tonight and I've kept you from it."

She shook her head, a cascade of curls breaking free from behind her shoulder and rushing to the front. She impatiently tucked them back. "I'm ready, and seriously, it was good, this time together. I wouldn't trade it for anything. You are right, though. We need to get a little rest before tomorrow." She chuckled and rose. I mirrored her, and we walked through the mostly deserted lounge and out into the brightly lit hallways. Maddie shielded her eyes with one hand as I squinted up at her.

"Whoa! That'll wake you right up," I murmured.

Maddie just shook her head, smiling as she pressed the elevator buttons. "Shall we meet at eight thirty? We can have breakfast before."

"Yes. Your topic sounds interesting. For tomorrow, I mean." Here I was, on eggshells again after spending such lovely quality time with her.

I could see her shift into professional mode, a small, subtle change. "So many mothers are refusing vaccinations for their children because they say it causes autism."

"But it doesn't, does it?" I asked, trying to remember if this had been addressed in my textbooks. We'd touched on it in class, but not to any great extent.

"We don't know what causes autism…" She paused as we entered the empty elevator car. "But, believe me, we don't want to go backward and create a world without vaccines. It would be horrific. There was an outbreak of mumps in California not too long ago. This is what is happening without the MMR vaccine for babies. Mumps can cause sterility in males." She shook her head.

"They don't think about that, though, do they? We've become a society that can't see beyond instant gratification."

"Exactly," she responded with a deep sigh. "This is what I'll be talking about tomorrow. Also, about the elderly who don't realize that there are many vaccines out there that can prevent ailments specific to their ages."

The elevator doors opened with a muted chime. We progressed along the carpeted hallway, and I felt as though she were holding my body against hers. As though a bubble of privacy, of intimacy, surrounded us. A fanciful notion, but she filled my senses completely.

We paused in front of our rooms.

"You're so smart," I said, apropos of nothing. I was awed by this woman, this physician.

"As are you," she said, her accent thick and melodious.

"I'm going to hug you," I said softly.

She moved very close. "I'd like that," she replied.

I was in her arms then, and it felt as though our hearts beat as one. I inhaled the subtle essence of her. She smelled like starch and lemon. I pressed my cheek to hers, wishing I could kiss her but not daring to. Her body was lean and firm, and I could feel the press of her breasts against mine, even though she was taller.

When we parted, I could see the blush staining her features.

"Goodnight Maddie," I said, looking away.

"*Buenas noches*, Ella," she replied, touching my hand briefly.

CHAPTER NINETEEN

Maddie

My presentation went well. I had a number of good graphics to help the roomful of attendees to understand how serious my topic had become during the past handful of years. My graph of future trends had turned out less than stellar, but I thought it was a satisfactory crystal ball for any who cared to believe.

I also had Ella, who watched both me and the audience with bright, contemplative eyes. I could see, in my own imagination, the gears of inspiration working in her mind. I looked forward to talking with her about the topic later in the day.

I finished to a roomful of applause, and Tom came by to congratulate me as I packed up my computer.

"Good job, as usual, Maddie," he said, shaking my hand. He then went on at exhaustive length about one mother he had dealt with who had absolutely refused any preventative treatment for her trio of very young children. He was rightfully concerned, but I had no easy answers. I finally suggested he put together a wake-up package that gave an overview—a photographic overview—of the preventable diseases that vaccines could prevent. His face brightened at that, and he hurried away.

"So, that must have been enlightening for him," Ella said as she approached. "What did you tell him?"

"Just a possible way to get some of his patients vaccinated." I shrugged. "Hope it works for him."

Ella was watching the last few attendees filing from the room. "That's our Doctor Maddie. Brilliant as always."

"Hmph," I offered doubtfully as I lifted my case.

I was remembering her at breakfast. She and I had both been giddy with excitement, perhaps excitement lingering from the previous night. It seemed as though we'd broken through some barrier to our psyches and could finally be at ease with one another. We'd snickered about pancakes shaped like the state of Alabama, discussed the merits of grape jelly and syrup as to which was the best topping for pancakes and agreed that vanilla soy lattes were the best way to drink our coffee.

"So, are we off to hear Quillen?" she asked as we walked toward the huge double doors.

I wrinkled my nose at her.

"What?" she queried, laughing.

"I slept enough last night," I told her. "One thing about Dr Quillen, his presentation is pretty much the same every year."

Ella pulled the program from her bag and folded it open to the speakers' page. "'New techniques for effective journaling to broaden patient care,'" she read aloud.

I sighed as we moved along the hallway. "Yep, that's the one. Let's see though, hmm. *New* techniques for journaling. Maybe that would be worth it," I murmured, index finger tapping my chin.

She chuckled. "It says here that encouraging your nursing staff to add entries is the key."

We looked at one another and laughed.

"So, what should we do instead?" she asked.

I had no idea. "What do you want to do?" I asked finally.

Her eyes lit. "Let's go up and change into jeans and sneakers. I have an idea."

Within half an hour, Ella and I were changed and out a side door of the hotel. We raced to my car and climbed inside. I took a deep breath and glanced at Ella. She was grinning, her gaze scouring the parking lot behind us.

"I think we made a clean getaway, boss," she said in a forties gangster's tone.

I laughed aloud. It did feel as though we were escaping the hotel. In reality, I knew we were escaping our traditional roles and the duties that bound us within those roles. I also knew we were on an adventure. I was excited, more excited than I had been in a very long time. Was this what life was like, life with a partner you felt at ease with? Could it always be this good? I was afraid to think about it too hard for fear of jinxing it somehow.

"So which way?" I asked as I pulled to the edge of the parking lot.

"Go right here," she said, consulting a scribbled map she held in her hand. I had noticed it in the elevator, but she had pulled it out of my sight. I surmised that our destination was a secret.

I turned right and followed the road for a few miles, at which point she directed me to turn left. We were heading closer into downtown Dothan.

"Turn right," she cried out, and I quickly executed a ninety-degree turn.

My mouth fell open and then a wide grin closed it. "No way!" I breathed.

Ella giggled. "Way! I knew you'd love it. I just knew!"

I parked quickly, and we rushed inside through an arched structure that resembled a huge, open clown mouth. The glass doors inside proclaimed: *Welcome! It's Time to Skate.* It certainly was.

We stood inside, both mesmerized as we absorbed the ambience of the huge skating rink. The familiar scents of popcorn and sugary candy assailed me, and I glanced to my left. Sure enough, there was a concession area with several small tables and a wall of narrow booths. To our right was the skate rental, a hut with an ultramodern spaceship theme. I glanced back at the rink. The brightly neon lit walls were painted with huge murals featuring superheroes, most notably from *The Incredibles*, a Pixar movie about a whole family of superheroes. I hadn't seen it, of course, but I had seen advertisements for it, including posters at my local grocery store back home.

"Oh my God, it's Jack-Jack!" Ella exclaimed.

I turned to her. "Who?"

"Isn't he cute? I just love that movie."

I followed her gaze and saw a single-toothed baby with a round head and a single spiky tuft for hair.

She was studying me. "You haven't seen it, have you?"

I grimaced an apology.

"Well, we'll remedy that as soon as we get home. I own it and we will definitely have a movie night. See there?" She pointed to a back mural and we moved closer to the waist-height rink wall to get a better view. "That's the father, the big man in the black mask. Same as over there, in the business suit—his alter ego." She grinned at me, and I was stunned by the grin's radiance.

She continued in my silence. "His name is Bob Parr. His superhero name is Mr. Incredible. That's his wife Helen next to him. Elastigirl when she's in the mask. The two older kids are Violet and Dash. She can be invisible, and he can move like lightning."

I cleared my throat. "So what do they *do*, in those fancy red leotards?"

She blinked slowly. "Well. Well, they save the world, silly. That guy there with the mop of fire hair is named Syndrome and he has some kind of old grudge against the Incredibles and he wants to wipe them out so he can take over the world."

"Ahh." I nodded my understanding.

She grinned sheepishly. "My favorite character is Edna, but I don't see her here. You'll see her. She designs the indestructible suits the superheroes wear and has more money than Croesus."

"Croesus?" I was drawing a blank.

She frowned at me. "You know, Greek guy, king. Lots of money."

I mentally raced through my Greek studies and vaguely recalled him. "Oh, yeah. Sorry." I knew I was blushing.

"No problem, Doc. Come on, let's skate!"

She grabbed my hand and pulled me toward the spaceship.

CHAPTER TWENTY

Ella

Roller-skating had always been a favorite activity of mine. When I was a little girl, my mother had often taken my sister and me to a tiny roller skating rink in a sport park outside Wiesbaden, Germany. Ice-skating was more popular in that area, but for some reason—probably her own nostalgia—my mother had chosen roller-skating as a fun activity she, Jess and I could do together while my father worked. I wasn't even sure that Maddie could skate, but for some weird reason, I had known she would enjoy doing this, whether she could skate or not. So I had taken the chance after admiring the rink in the brochure the previous day.

"Do you have any idea how long it's been since I've had on roller skates?" Maddie said as she tightened the laces on her rentals, size nine. Mine were size eight and a half, and I had already finished fastening them snugly.

"It's been a while for me too," I responded. "I guess we can hold one another up, if need be."

She eyed me archly. "All I have to say is, if I go down, you're going with me." She laughed and rose, wobbling, to her feet. I rose too and grabbed her arm as a sloping floor seemed to pull us toward the rink. We both slammed into the wall next to the rink opening, and I started to laugh.

Maddie studied me, as if trying to keep a stern face. She was rubbing an elbow that she'd hit on the wall. Watching her pretend austerity cracked me up even further, so I laughed until I was breathless. Within seconds, she had joined in, and we stood there making spectacles of ourselves. People had been staring already, simply because we weren't locals, now they had even more to gawk at. Eventually, the hilarity subsided into small coughs and sniffles.

"Are you done?" Maddie asked, still chortling helplessly but trying to control it.

"Yes," I managed to gasp. "I think so."

She chuckled and took in a deep breath. "So...so we can skate now?"

I nodded, not even looking at her for fear of losing composure again. I focused on my feet as I stepped into the rink, still clutching the wall and pulling myself along. I could feel her right behind me. We circled that way for a few minutes as I watched the local skaters whiz by us.

"They go awfully fast," Maddie said through clenched teeth.

I felt laughter well up again. "Yes. Yes, they do."

"Ella?"

"Yes Maddie?"

"Is there a kiddie rink somewhere that we should be in?"

That did it—I was gone. As I bent, laughing, my feet flew out from under me, and I landed on my backside, curled double with merriment.

"Are you okay?" Maddie asked when she could squeeze words out from between her own gurgles of laughter. She hovered above me as I tried to catch my breath.

"You girls all right?" asked an elderly woman as she skated up to us.

"We...ah..." Maddie broke into stifled laughter again.

The woman smiled at us, revealing two gold teeth to the left of her front incisors. Her salt-and-pepper hair was cropped close, and her broad mahogany features were curious but accepting.

"Y'all just ain't got no sense, that's what it is," she said in a motherly tone. "Have either of you girls even been on skates befo'?"

"Actually, we have," Maddie said. "But it seems like we just can't stop laughing long enough to stay on our feet."

I held up an arm and the stranger grabbed my forearm as Maddie grabbed my upper arm. They lifted me up, and I rolled slowly toward the wall as I wiped tears from my eyes with my fingers.

"I'm sorry, ma'am," I said. "I just get so tickled sometimes."

"It's Ethel, young 'un. I been workin' here for nigh on thirty year now, and I'd be glad to help y'all get over to the center where there's a little less traffic, if you like."

"I think we need that, Ethel," Maddie said. The laughter had finally gone out of her voice, though there was still a small tinge of amusement.

I nodded my agreement, and Ethel took each of us by the crook of an elbow and, timing it just right, pulled us through the circling skaters on the outer perimeter. She skated, still linked with us, for a few minutes, circling the inner perimeter, around where the few really good skaters were practicing their moves. Soon I felt the familiar rhythm of skating return, and when a Bee Gees song sounded all around us, I was able to skate to its disco beat. I looked over at Maddie and found her smiling into the wind, eyes closed as she moved along with the familiar strokes as well.

"There you go, girls," Ethel shouted. She handed Maddie's hand to me and then she drifted away, into the crowd. Maddie smiled at me and squeezed my hand. We continued to skate together without problem.

I reveled in the well-remembered patterns of movement as I let the music swell inside and fill me completely. It just felt so damned good to move into the wind, neon lights and bright, energizing colors surrounding us. The music was good, too, not as cheesy as in some rinks I'd been in. The pipe organ music was a dim memory as Top 40 hits mingled with disco and a few nineties hits filled the rink. The skaters that passed us were smiling, some showing off practiced moves that reminded me of ballet. One older couple glided by as if ballroom dancing.

I glanced at Maddie and fell in love with her anew. Her dark curls were streaming back, rioting against their sedate, careful lives. She still held my hand, even though it made the sashay more difficult for both of us. I didn't think she cared, and I knew I didn't. I honestly wished we could stay here forever.

CHAPTER TWENTY-ONE

Maddie

I had forgotten how much I loved roller-skating. It had been one of my favorite activities when, as a child and young teen, I had gone with my mother to the Empire, a beautiful old rink in central Brooklyn. It had been especially fun when my mother's brother, Umberto, had visited from Puerto Rico. Though he'd spoken very little English, he'd been fascinated with all things American and had boogied to the seventies music with amazing aplomb. I had loved those times.

Now, as I glided next to the woman I was quickly learning to adore, I fully realized that some things are so ingrained in you when young that you never quite forget how to do them. A sense of relief filled me, and I finally realized that yes, I could love again. Fear had paralyzed me for so long as I endeavored to move ahead in my career that it had been easy to ignore basic human needs. I was skating that fear away, and it fell from me in huge chunks. The voids that were left filled with brightness, and I was infused with joy.

I looked at Ella and reveled in her obvious joy. Releasing some of the pent-up tension that had been building between us was a good thing for both of us.

The crowd had died down somewhat, and I checked my watch. It was past five o'clock. I shook my head in amazement as I pulled Ella closer.

"It's quarter past five," I said as I leaned toward her ear.

Her eyes widened. "We've been here almost five hours?"

I grinned and patted her hand, which I had tucked into my elbow. "Hard to believe, isn't it? I guess time does fly when you are having fun."

She smiled at me and covered my hand with hers.

"And I am having fun," I assured her.

"Me, too," she said, and then sighed. "Guess we'd better get back."

She gently pulled me to the side, and it was only then that I realized how sore my knees and ankles were. So much for reliving my youth.

"Ouch!" Ella said as we hobbled toward the opening. "I think every muscle in my body hurts. Thank goodness we took that break for the slice of pizza or it might even be worse!"

I groaned, expressing my own pain. "Surely it couldn't be any worse. What were we thinking, skating like this at our ages?"

"I don't know if it's so much an age thing. More like an out-of-shape thing." Continuing to hold the wall, Ella swung her body around to the outside of the rink and pigeon-stepped toward the padded benches. I followed suit. We sat silent, side by side, for a long beat, both grinning like fools.

"It *was* fun, wasn't it?" Ella asked finally. She lifted an eyebrow and looked at me questioningly. I felt as though her nervousness was returning, eclipsing the joy of the afternoon. I wanted to put her at ease.

"The best time I've had in ten years," I told her, taking her hand in mine. I let my thumb caress the soft skin on the back of her hand. Our eyes connected, and I felt myself pulled in to her lips. I studied their plump pinkness, knowing I was going to kiss her. Then I came to my senses and pulled back. I wanted to, desperately, but couldn't look into her eyes again. I knew that if I did, I *would* kiss her, and it was just too soon. We hadn't even talked seriously about our sexual preferences. How could I just assume she was a lesbian? How could I know for sure that she was attracted to me? I released her hand and bent forward to untie my skates. "Maybe we could do this again sometime? I wonder if there's a rink near home that we could visit."

Ella was silent a long beat. I prayed I hadn't offended her by my presumptuousness. I needed to move more slowly, to see if her feelings for me could develop. I glanced at her and found her studying me thoughtfully. "Ella?"

She shook her head as if to clear it. "I honestly don't know, but I will certainly be checking that out as soon as we get home." She grinned. "Especially now that I have a partner in my lunacy."

I was held in the tractor beam of her smile, and my fingers fumbled at the laces. "Yes. It sounds like a lot of fun," I said, looking away and focusing on pulling off a skate. I wiggled my toes, enjoying the freedom and the fresh air.

"Feels good, doesn't it?" Ella asked with a giggle.

I nodded and pulled off the other skate. I stood and held out my hand to her. "Can you stand?"

She grimaced as though I were foolish. "Of course, silly." She rose, but a groan did escape her lips.

"Mmhm," I muttered.

I let her lead the way as we traveled the short distance to the rental kiosk.

Moments later, we were in the car headed back through downtown Dothan in the direction of the hotel.

"I hope no one has missed us," I said.

Ella sighed. "It is rather irresponsible to take you away from the conference. But you did seem to want to get away."

"I did, yes. Today was absolutely perfect. If we were missed, we were missed. I really don't care."

She giggled. "Well, we *are* adults, I suppose, and don't always have to do as we're told."

I laughed with her. "Ella, I'm not quite sure two mature adults would spend a handful of hours skating as blissfully and deliriously as we did."

She glanced at me, her expression surprised. "Why, of course we would," she said slowly. "Why wouldn't we?"

I looked at the heavy traffic as I mulled this. Indeed. Why wouldn't we? I knew with new certainty that Ella would bring only positive things into my life.

CHAPTER TWENTY-TWO

Ella

I took a final look at myself in the well-lit bathroom mirror. I would do.

I had taken a long, hot shower when we'd returned to the hotel, which had refreshed me and eased some of the sore muscles. I didn't even want to think about the stiffness the morning would bring.

Tonight, for dining, I had chosen to wear the soft linen trousers my sister had recommended. They were a dark taupe color, and I topped them with a coffee-colored tank and a long, sheer black cardigan that was mostly lace. My jewelry was simple: small earrings and a long necklace, both featuring golden circles of amber. I might have been hurting, but no one would know. I smiled at myself and, after grabbing my bag, left the room.

Maddie's door opened right after my knock. She looked refreshed, dressed in her usual crisp white button-down shirt, with a dark-blue linen blazer and loose trousers. Her hair was down, and it curled gently on her shoulders. She was beautiful.

"Hi. How do you feel?" I asked.

"Better than before," she said. "Are you ready for a drink?"

"You betcha." I smiled.

She stepped into the hall and pulled the door closed. She looked at me sideways. "You look really beautiful tonight. You'll have to carry a big stick to beat the suitors off."

"Suitors? What a lovely, old-fashioned word," I said. "No, I have no interest in other suitors."

I hoped that she would understand my meaning. She didn't comment on it, and we walked silently to the elevator.

The lobby was just as crowded as the night before. The conference really wouldn't end until midday Tuesday, so most likely all the attendees were still in the hotel. We waded into the fray, Maddie following close behind me. I led us to the bar, sensing that we would need fortitude to deal with another press of Maddie's peers.

"I think you two are deliberately avoiding me," said Dixie as she approached us, a tall pink cocktail in one hand. "I came by your room to ask you if you wanted an afternoon swim, but there was no answer."

"We were seeing downtown," Maddie said before turning away and ordering our drinks.

"Ahh, downtown's lovely," she said. She swayed slightly, and I wondered how many drinks she'd had. I leaned close.

"Are you okay, Dixie?" I asked quietly.

"Never better," she said, smiling in a lopsided way.

Maddie returned and handed me my vodka and grapefruit. "Let's file in for dinner, you two," she suggested.

She took my arm and unexpectedly extended an elbow to Dixie, who, though she appeared surprised, accepted the gesture. We moved into the haphazardly populated dining room.

"Excuse me," Dixie muttered as she broke away and headed unsteadily toward two young women standing to one side.

Maddie sighed as if in relief and drew me toward a table near the mostly empty back of the room. "Okay if we sit back here?" she asked.

"Are you hiding from someone?" I asked, amused, as I slid onto a chair. I placed my drink in front of me and then took a deep sip of it. It was cold, refreshing and just the right amount of bitter.

"I think everyone," Maddie replied as she sat and scrubbed at her forehead with both hands.

I touched her forearm, suddenly concerned. "Are you okay, hon? Do you feel badly?"

"No. No, I'm fine." She turned her head and smiled up at me, head still in her hands. She sat back suddenly and took a slow sip of her scotch. "Ella?"

"Yes Maddie?"

"I find myself wondering about you," she said quietly.

"Hmm. How do you mean?" I was curious about her line of thinking.

She squirmed uncomfortably. "I...I guess I want to know what...well, what you want."

"What I want?" I lifted my drink and took a slow, calming swallow. "That's easy."

"Why are you two sitting back here?" Dixie asked as she bumped into our table and then seated herself. "It's all shadowy and gloomy, and there's no one to talk to."

"That's sort of the point," Maddie said with some ill humor.

"Hmm?" Dixie didn't understand in her somewhat inebriated condition.

"We're just worn out from today," I said, trying to smooth things.

Dixie fiddled with her empty glass and sighed loudly. "Well, I have to sit over there. Mama says." She flopped one hand toward the front of the room. "Come sit with us, if you want."

"Looks like your table is filling pretty quickly," Maddie said with an indicating nod.

Dixie glanced nonchalantly in the direction Maddie had indicated. She rose and grunted. "Shame it won't fill completely. I'm just about bored out of my skull, listening to all those old prunes talk about medicine this, medicine that."

I grimaced at Maddie and pushed Dixie's empty glass to one side as Maddie leaned forward. "It's easy? Why easy?"

I blushed and took in a deep breath, preparing myself. Once the words were out, they'd be out. I wouldn't be able to take them back.

"Would you liked iced tea, ma'am?" the young server asked as she offered the steel pitcher with both hands.

Maddie leaned back, expelling her breath.

"Yes, please," I responded. I glanced around and noticed that the waitstaff was already serving dinner.

"Maddie? Tea for you?" I asked.

She glanced at the server and nodded. Another of the waitstaff approached behind her, bearing plates of food. As the first girl left us, the second server, a young man with cropped blond hair, placed our food on the table.

We sat silently looking at the plates for almost a minute.

"Here's bread for you," a third server said. "Let us know if you need anything."

She placed the basket of towel-wrapped bread between our plates, toward the center of the table.

We still didn't move.

Finally, Maddie shifted in her chair. "Ella? I—"

I lifted my drink and took one more deep swallow. "It's you, Maddie. It's you I want."

CHAPTER TWENTY-THREE

Maddie

My heart was beating rapidly in my chest. I actually wondered if I might be having a heart attack. She'd said it. She'd made her intentions clear. My psyche soared, and I felt a happiness fill me, making me complete in places deep within that I hadn't realized were empty. I wanted to take her hand, but hers were both on the table, and I didn't want to be too obvious.

"Ella, think about what you are saying," I said quietly.

"Are you telling me that you have no feelings for me?" Her question was filled with doubt, so I hastened to reassure her.

"Of course I do. I've had feelings for you since the day you came to work for me."

She turned to face me head on. "Why didn't you say anything? I was never sure how you felt."

I dropped my eyes and leaned to touch her knee with my fingertips. "I was so afraid."

"Of me?"

"No…well, maybe. But I was more afraid of allowing myself to feel, I think. It's easy to ignore what's missing in your life if you pretend you can't feel anything."

She smiled impishly. "Then I come along and prove to be absolutely irresistible."

I studied her beautiful, beloved features. "Yes, yes. Exactly like that."

She smiled again, her eyes soft and loving. "I figured it was an ethical thing, you avoiding all my advances."

"You mean not fraternizing with my employees?"

"Yes." She nodded. "Is that true?"

"Yes, very true. That gave me much pause. *Pero te necesito tanto.*" She watched me questioningly, so I explained in a low whisper. "I need you, Ella. I need you so very much." I waited nervously.

"And I need you. I won't hesitate to find another job, Maddie. I want to…if it means we can be together."

Relieved, I leaned close, finally taking both her hands in mine. "We will be together, Ella. Never doubt that. Please. No matter what. Never doubt that."

She smiled at me, tears welling in her eyes. "I've waited so long to hear those words from you."

"Stay here. I'll be right back."

A wonderful idea had occurred to me, and I hurried out to the lobby bar. I placed an order with the grinning bartender and then rushed back to my love. "Will you come with me?" I said, sliding back into my chair. I watched her face. Would she trust me?

"But your dinner—" she said with some surprise.

"I'm…not hungry. For food."

She smiled. "Okay. We'll find you something later."

She rose and we left the dining room and made our way to the elevator. We were silent, but there was a heady energy humming between us as we rode up. At the doors to our rooms, I took her hand and propelled her toward mine. When the door closed behind us, I turned to face her in the dim light of the room, placing a palm on each of her rosy cheeks.

"Ella, *tu haces que mi corazón se eleva y se llena con luz,*" I whispered. "*Ven sé conmigo ahora.*"

She moved closer to me, only a breath apart. "Yes, whatever you said, yes."

"I said you make my heart soar and fill it with light. Come, be with me now." I wrapped her in my arms, allowed at last to hold her soft flesh next to mine. I reveled in it, breathing in her essence, our noses touching. She was delectable, better than I'd hoped. Slowly, savoring every move, I closed the distance until I permitted myself, at last, to press my lips to hers.

In my mind, I shifted to another dimension. Her lips were plump and warm, and I was drawn in, my tongue plundering the sweet depths of her mouth. This same mouth had driven me crazy as I'd watched it speak to me in the past. This new dimension moved me past being spoken *to*. Now I was spoken *with*. This new, nonverbal language filled my brain with incredible peace and excitement in equal measure. I pulled her body ever closer, crushing her to me, wanting her to experience fully this same dimension. We were time travelers, creating bold and utopic worlds as we traveled through them. Warmth suffused me as I allowed my physical hands to reach low and fill with her grounding flesh so we would stay anchored together somehow.

I wasn't sure how long we traveled in this merged state, but an insistent knock at the door slammed me back into this reality. We broke apart too abruptly, almost painfully.

"It's for us," I said lamely, my chest heaving. I turned on one small desk lamp and smoothed my clothing, knowing I could do nothing to change the dreaminess of my facial expression. After opening the door, I ushered in the young woman who pushed a roomservice cart. I fished my wallet out of my pocket and tipped her, and she wished us a good evening as she left.

I turned to Ella and found her cheeks bright pink and her mouth curved in a Mona Lisa secretive smile. "Wine?"

"Yes," she said, nodding. "After that kiss, I need it."

I chuckled. "Our chemistry is strong, yes?" I handed her a full glass. "This is a Muscat grape, very pleasant, usually."

She took a sip and raised surprised eyes above her glass. "This is like nectar," she whispered.

I nodded and savored my own wine. "Yes, it is my favorite. We have these grapes in Puerto Rico, in the southwestern region. They are in a popular local wine there, even better than this, and I always try to visit the village for a good meal and some of the wine there whenever I go back."

Ella walked the few steps that separated us and took my hand, then pulled me toward the bed. We sat next to one another on the edge.

"Do you think I could go with you sometime? To Puerto Rico?" she asked softly.

"Of course you will," I replied, lifting my glass to hers in a toast. "To our timeless future, filled with one another."

She smiled at my toast and took a deep sip of the petit grain Moscatel.

"Maddie, have you been in many relationships?" she asked, with what appeared to be reluctance.

"Not many," I admitted. "I know I should have had more at my age, but my work was my mistress. My last was with a woman when I was in medical school. She treated me badly. Before that I had a few girlfriends, briefly, when I was very young." I moved to refill our glasses. "And you? Tell me about your loves."

"Not so many," she replied. "My first real girlfriend was in high school, Katrina Merkel. We had to keep it secret, of course, and she eventually left me for one of my nerdy male classmates. I came out to everyone when I was in college, when I fell in love with a girl named Gina. I thought she was everything I wanted, but she fell in love with another. I was brokenhearted, in that tormented way of youth, so I rebelled against everything, eventually hooking up with a woman named Bailey, who my parents really hated. She and I got in lots of trouble until she went away."

I could see Ella's pain, but it wasn't all consuming. That was good. I stood and took her glass, returning both our glasses to the cart. I took off my blazer.

"Come," I said, pulling her to her feet. She smiled seductively as I removed her light jacket. "Now, you are mine," I said, my lips finding her fragrant, warm neck. "And I am yours."

CHAPTER TWENTY-FOUR

Ella

I felt as though my heart would stop beating as Maddie began to make love to me. Her touch was so gentle, so ethereal, that it all felt dreamlike. My clothing fell from me, and I felt no inhibition being naked and honest before her. Her large hands swept my skin, the palms soft and hot as she explored— no, delighted in my body. Fingers, strong but gentle, caressed my neck up into my hairline, and I discovered this to be a new erogenous zone for me. And always there was her mouth, consuming my lips, her powerful tongue following her hands in worship of my nape as I rolled to accommodate her. One hand lowered and found my breasts, erect and firm, and a whole new spate of sensations wrapped me in delirium. Fluid swelled in me, the apex of my legs twitching in anticipation of penetration, of release.

One hand still cupped my head and neck as I was kissed. And kissed yet again. The other hand abandoned my breasts and slid along my torso, pressing securely against my ribs, my waist, then moving along the full cheek of my bottom, pressing my center against her firm body. A new fount of moisture filled me, and I gasped at the extreme sensation she aroused. I pulled back and looked into her eyes. I found love there and deep, dark passion. What I saw was almost more sensation than I could bear, and I trembled.

"Tell me this is real, Maddie," I whispered shakily.

She breathed out and nibbled my lips before whispering a reply. "This is real, *mi canto*. More real than anything before. We are creating a new reality. We generate new life and light between us."

I rolled onto my back, pulling her with me. I reached to unbutton her shirt, my fingers fumbling the task. Maddie rose to her knees and swept the shirt off over her head. Her undershirt followed, and I saw her unfettered leanness for the first time. Her tan skin seemed to glow with an inner light. Her breasts were small and sloped upward, the nipples small and dark. Her unbound curls cascaded wildly across her shoulders as if teasing those breasts. It was a sight I knew I would remember the rest of my life.

I reached upward and pressed both palms to the space just below her breasts, spreading my fingers outward across her pronounced ribs. She unfastened her trousers and then lowered her body atop mine. There were those mesmerizing kisses again, pulling me from this world, easily thrusting me into another sensual realm where time and place ceased to exist. I shuddered, closer to orgasm than I'd ever been without benefit of touch.

"Oh, Maddie. Oh, *Maddie*," I murmured, pulling one of her thighs between my legs. She understood and pressed upward, even as her hand clutched my hip for more control. Her mouth left mine as she threw back her head and groaned. Her sandalwood-scented hair brushed my cheek as she turned her head, eyes closed. I pressed my lips to her neck, nibbling the corded skin there.

Her hand left my hip and crept between us, the fingers easily finding and penetrating my throbbing center. She moved slightly to one side, and as her mouth found my lips again, the heel of her palm pressed against my hard, protruding clit. A few strokes in and out and I was done. My body arched off the bed as I wailed into Maddie's mouth and my world exploded. My toes curled and my thighs tingled and quivered. I muttered nonsensical words as I tried to find my way back to reality. Maddie's hand had thankfully stilled, but it remained, surely feeling my intense contractions of pleasure.

I tried to be embarrassed but didn't have the wherewithal to *be* anything but a quivering mass of sensual reverberation.

Maddie gently kissed along my chest, above my breasts. I closed my eyes, feeling her against me, smelling her beautiful scent. I managed to lift the arm stretched behind her, and I pulled her closer with it. She nestled into me, with small mews of comfort. Her hand slid from me, and she rested it on the bed next to my side as she embraced me fully, one thigh across mine. We lay that way a very long time, connecting, until the air conditioning came on and chilly air swept across us.

Maddie rose and slid from her trousers and panties. She loosened the sheets and blankets, tucking me into them. She slid in next to me and held me close, nose to nose.

"At last," she sighed.

"At last," I replied. "No more doubt?"

"No more doubt. No fear."

She kissed me deeply, and I felt a new fire kindle. I cupped one of her breasts in my hand. "You're so beautiful," I whispered, leaning to press my lips to the soft flesh there. She sighed and rolled to lie on her back.

"Love me, Ella," she ordered quietly as she spread her arms in invitation.

"Oh, I will," I assured her. I took her nipple between my lips and tongued it, relishing in how it grew unbelievably hard under my attention. Maddie moaned, and I captured the other, teasing it in similar fashion. She had her eyes closed, but I could see her skin pinken in anticipation. I moved back and forth between her breasts for a slow, unmeasured time, until she whimpered her need. Only then did I move lower, kissing that gorgeous expanse of skin until I reached a forest of curly dark hair. I brushed it with my fingers, lightly, slowly. I had no desire for this interlude to end. Even temporarily. Why couldn't lovers love one another all the time? Why did jobs and other people have to interfere?

I moved a knee between Maddie's thighs and lowered myself below the blankets. As I flattened to my stomach and pressed my lips to her quivering upper thigh, I understood. To do so, to do this all the time, would be a type of madness. A madness spawned from pleasure. One the human psyche just couldn't endure.

CHAPTER TWENTY-FIVE

Maddie

Breakfast had been a tempest of delight. Though we had to keep our newfound relationship secret, for work purposes, still everything was very different. I wondered if my peers would notice, so I made a real effort not to meet Ella's eyes when around them. But the energy, the pervasive chemistry we emitted…I wasn't sure how anyone could have missed that. Nor the dopey, happy grins.

Now, on the way home, I cleared my throat and squeezed the hand I'd been holding as I drove. "So, Sandy will know, won't she?"

Ella sighed and shrugged. "I'm not sure how she wouldn't. Did you see how strangely Dixie was eyeing us at breakfast? I'm sure she's guessed."

"You…um, you really didn't want to date her, did you?"

"Of course not, you beautiful woman. I only have eyes for you. Though…" She paused, and my heart lurched. "I did consider it, for the briefest second, when you seemed to be persistently ignoring my advances."

"There's no way I could have ignored you any longer. I was going just a little crazy." I stroked her hand with my thumb. "I'll never make that mistake again. I can promise you that."

She smiled tenderly at me and then turned to study the passing landscape. "So, what about Sandy?"

"I've been giving this a lot of thought and, you know, everyone will need to know, sooner or later. I mean, I plan to stay in Maypearl and practice. And—"

She turned and eyed me curiously. "And?"

I took a deep breath. "And of course I want you in my life. To be with me."

I felt the radiance coming from her rather than saw it. "Do you mean that?" she asked breathlessly.

I checked the traffic all around and managed to pull to the side of the interstate. I put the SUV in park and turned to her. "Ella, I don't know you as well as I plan to know you, but I am certain of the way I feel when I am with you. You…yes, you fill my heart with light. I've never had that before, so I'm not well-versed in this committed relationship thing. But I want, no, plan to try being a couple. I want to come home to you, or with you, every day and discuss our days. The way we feel about our days. I want to hold you at night while we sleep and wake with you as I did this morning." I paused and took in a deep breath. "I hope you feel the same way, and I think you do. If not, let's discuss it."

She nodded. "And we could, you know. Discuss it. I don't think there's anything we can't talk about. At least now." She grinned at me. "So, shall we? Play house together?"

Relief filled me. "Yes! Yes, please."

She unbuckled her seat belt and pressed her lips to mine. Heat surged through me, and I felt desire for her start at the end of my spine and work its way upward. Time passed uncounted as we lost ourselves in one another. When I found myself straining against my seat belt, trying to possess her, I pulled away and laughed shakily. "Ah, woman. What you do to me is…well, it just *is*."

She wasn't unfazed. I watched her chest rise and fall as she straightened her blouse. She chuckled. "Let's get home, my love."

"Together," I added as I carefully pulled back onto the highway.

For the next two hours, we discussed logistics. She still wanted to leave the practice, and I was begging her to stay. For some reason, working together would not be a conflict for me any longer. I wasn't sure why my viewpoint had changed, but now I imagined us working together as an even more streamlined medical team. Her doubts were sound, but in the euphoria of our new love, I couldn't see us working apart from one another. We tabled that decision for a later discussion.

Another discussion concerned where we would live. I didn't care at all, trusting that she would make wherever we lived a cozy, personalized abode for the two of us. She remained undecided, however, and I guessed giving up her independence, via her apartment, was proving hard for her. I felt sad about that but certainly understood it. I let her know right away that Julio would be a welcome addition to our new family. I was actually excited about the idea of having a pet again.

I squelched a sudden niggle of doubt at one point. My evenings, although lonely, were when I was safely able to think and to spend time writing and studying. I was apprehensive of what I imagined would be a certain amount of chaos in my future. I knew Ella was an avid reader. We'd make it work.

Seeing the large blue sign welcoming us back to Maypearl set a whole new wheel of apprehension into motion. How would my patients react to Ella being my partner, maybe one day my wife? What would change in my career? A glow of peace filled me as I realized I just didn't care. I couldn't care. Being as unhappy and unfulfilled as I'd been since meeting Ella and not having her as my love had revealed to me that a happy woman made a happier doctor. I'd be a better physician with Ella in my life. This was a fact, as far as I was concerned. The patients and Sandy would just have to come around. It might be uncomfortable in the beginning but, really, wasn't I allowed to have a loving, fulfilled life?

I pulled into a parking space near the door to Ella's apartment. I carried both our bags inside.

Julio greeted us with loud complaints with a few 'welcome home's thrown in, just to be politically correct. Ella seemed to be listening to him, deciphering his language, and I thought she was adorable the way she tilted her ear toward him, listening with intense concentration.

"Yes, yes. I know Sandy was here. You don't think I'd leave you all by yourself, do you? Did she feed you what you wanted?"

I fell under the spell myself, swearing I could make out words in the jumble of mews and meows.

"Well, I'll tell her not so much salmon next time," Ella said as they walked down the hall to the bedroom. I followed as a smiling bellman, a small suitcase in each hand.

"You can just put them on the bed," she said, and it took me a minute to realize she was talking to me.

"Ah, so it's okay if I stay here tonight?"

She sidled close and insinuated her body against mine. I leaned my head forward. She captured my lips and thoroughly answered my question.

CHAPTER TWENTY-SIX

Ella

As soon as Maddie left to check out things at the office, I went back into the living room and dialed my sister.

"Jess! Jess! Jess!" I cried out as she answered.

"Whoa! Hold up, Auntie El, it's Westie. Are you okay?" I could hear the concern in her voice, so I calmed myself.

"Of course, sweetie. How are you?"

"Superfragicool. Mom made Dad cough up the dough for a new microscope so I can sweep my finals so, yeah, all is suweet!"

I laughed at her youthful enthusiasm about a microscope, of all things. "That sounds amazing. What are you working on?"

We talked shop until my sister sounded in the background and Westie told her I was on the phone. Westie signed off, and I heard Jess.

"Ella? How was your trip?" she asked. "I want all the details. Fess up."

I was held spellbound, making fish-kiss noises into the phone.

"Ella? *Ella?*" She sounded panicky.

"It happened," I wheezed out. "She…she *loves* me."

"Oh, Ella," she sighed.

"And wants to *live* with me. Like, forever!"

Jess squealed into the phone and, of course, I matched her squeal for squeal as Julio eyed me with disgust.

"Oh, sis. I am so incredibly happy for you. Is she wonderful? Did you…?"

I grinned and poked Julio impudently. "Yes. Last night, and let's say…well, I can't keep my hands off her. She is so very luscious."

"Lus-cious," Jess repeated, drawing out the word. "That sounds so wonderful for you. Oh my God. So, when can I meet her? Oh, and what about the job? Will you keep working there?"

I curled into the sofa next to Julio, scooting him over. He grumbled but moved easily enough. "We're still talking about that. She wants me to, but…"

"But?" I heard the sliding glass door through the phone and could picture her walking out to sit on the expansive deck Brian had built for her. The chair cushions blew out air as she sat.

"I don't know why I have reservations. I guess it goes back to my gut feeling about asking her to break, what? Protocol? I just don't want to be responsible if she…thinks about that someday."

"I get that. Maybe not such a bad idea."

"But then I think about the two of us working *together*, you know, like as a *team*. That excites me. We'd be like Batman and Robin. The Lone Ranger and Tonto."

Jess laughed so hard that she choked and fell into a coughing fit. This set me off, and we cackled together like two old hens.

"Oh, Ella," she sighed finally. "Be happy, hon. You certainly deserve it, and I am so very happy for you. I'm sure the two of you will make all the right decisions. Life is too short not to, you know?"

"Yeah," I replied thoughtfully. "And she's so wonderfully, well, together. I know I can trust her to make the right decisions for us. Hey, did I tell you her family is from Puerto Rico? That's kind of weird, isn't it? I've never dated anyone like her. Oh, and

Jess, you should hear her speak Spanish, it makes me like, um, Gomez with Morticia on *The Adams Family* movie."

Jess laughed. "Oh, so you mean you want to kiss her all up her arm and utter sweet nothings to her every time she speaks it?"

"Yeah," I blushed, hoping Julio wouldn't notice. "Something like that."

"Oh, El, you got it so bad, and I'm loving this living it again through you. You just wait, two years from now, you'll be bitching about something she does that gets on your nerves."

"Yeah, probably. Everything's like that, I know. But right now she's got me wrapped around her little finger. I can't wait for you to meet her."

"Maybe you guys could drive up next month for our anniversary party. Twenty-five years."

"Damn! It's been that long?"

"I know." She sighed. "Hard to believe. We've been lucky, I guess. No reasons to split. We don't even fight. Guess we'll be like Mom and Dad and just grow old together."

"But you're okay with that, right?" I asked.

"Absolutely. I can't imagine anyone I'd rather grow old with. Maybe you and your Maddie will be the same way. I'm crossing my fingers."

I thought about that a long moment. Yes, Maddie and I would be perfect as two old ladies living and loving together.

"El?"

"Sorry, woolgathering. So, when should I tell Mom and Dad? And Barbie?"

I could sense Jessica's shrug. "Who cares? I wouldn't rush it. You don't have to see them until next Christmas, if then. It's your life, and they have no say over it."

"I'd sorta like to let them know that I can be a lesbian and still be happy," I murmured.

"No, you just want to prove them wrong. What will that get you, Ella?"

Damn Jess. She was always so reasonable. "Satisfaction," I said sarcastically. "No, I know. Not the best motive. I hear you."

"Mmhm," she responded doubtfully.

I laughed. "Look, gotta go. I want to unpack before she gets back."

"Where'd she go?"

"Just to the office to make sure everything's okay. And to relieve the relief doc for tomorrow."

"So, what *are* you gonna do about work?"

"I'll go in and probably give notice tomorrow. We'll see. She's coming back here tonight, and maybe we'll talk about it some more then."

"Okay, lil sis, love you bunches," she said, signing off.

"Love you back," I replied before ending the connection.

Julio stretched against my leg, drawing my attention. "So, what do you think, little man? Should I find another job? I sure can't make up my mind."

He stared at me and blinked one eye slowly.

"That's no help," I told him. "Let Mama up so I can make everything perfect for when my woman-love comes home."

He turned his head away, and I wriggled out from under his substantial weight.

"Yeah, I know, cheesy. Just can't help myself," I told him, giggling as I traveled the hall to the bedroom.

CHAPTER TWENTY-SEVEN

Maddie

"So, how was the office?" she asked me when I seated myself at the table. I couldn't answer right away. I was still tingling and stunned by the warm kisses she'd greeted me with just moments ago. Being in a relationship with Ella was certainly going to change my life in the most pleasant of ways.

Finally finding my voice, I answered her. "It was good. Jason has everything under control."

She turned from the counter. "When is Dr Mikas leaving?"

I studied the feast before me. She'd made a huge bowl of salad, covered it with a layer of roasted nuts and then prepared a platter of crusty, buttery bread to go with it. "After he closes the office today. This looks so good. Thank you for doing this."

"You're welcome, my darling. I thought a salad a good idea as I had veggies that needed to be used up. And bread, of course." She seated herself and smiled at me. "Enjoy."

I dug in with gusto, realizing how famished I'd become since our late breakfast. I realized after several moments of silence that Ella was watching me eat. I laughed and covered my mouth with one hand. "Stop that," I said. "You're making me self-conscious."

Her eyes held adoration in their depths, and I wondered that I had never seen anyone look at me with that type of affection before. How could I have lived all these years without that in my life?

"Ah, *Dios mio*," I whispered.

"What?" she said, head tilting to one side. She held a slice of bread upraised in one hand.

"When you look at me like that, I realize that there is so much more to life than food."

"Such as?" Her tone was light and flirty, but there was a serious undertone to her query.

"Love. Love such as we have between us. I can't believe it's taken me so long to find it."

"And for that, I'm glad," she said, shrugging. "Otherwise, it would be my loss."

I nodded and we resumed our meal in silence. Julio meowed loudly, and Ella reached to smooth the heavy fur on his back.

"Did you eat a lot of salads growing up?" she asked thoughtfully sometime later.

I shook my head. "Unfortunately, no. My mother was a traditional cook. We ate *plantanos*, avocado, rice, beans, pork. For breakfast, I often had *pan de leche* with a little olive oil and salt."

She watched me as if fascinated. "So, very little meat, then?"

I chewed on a thin slice of red pepper. "Very little meat. Pork simmered in garlic and peppers. Served with beans over rice. Delicious. I'll make it for you one day."

"I'd like that." She took my hand and held it. "I am so looking forward to getting to know you, everything about you."

I chuckled and started quietly singing "Getting to Know You" from *The King and I*. She laughed and playfully pushed my hand away as if miffed.

"I do."

I rose and moved to her. I pulled her to her feet and hitched our bodies close together. We stood that way, nose to nose, breathing one another's air. I smelled nuts and lettuce, and garlic from the dressing. Her eyes were a calm, rich green as I gazed into them. They seemed pensive, and I wondered what she was thinking.

"Can we ever really know another?" I whispered. "Yet I want to share all of me with you. I want to know you, as well."

She cupped my face in her hands. "We can only know what we trust to share. And we'll have a lifetime. There's no rush. Trust will build in time."

"There's my sensible love." I moved back and took both her hands in mine. "I can't promise it will always be easy. Medicine has always been my life. Sometimes you may have to be patient with me."

She grinned widely and began unbuttoning her shirt. "Maybe I should practice getting your attention. All work and no play makes Maddie a dull, dull doctor."

I allowed her to pull me along the hall. "I see you've learned your medical assisting lessons very well."

She paused abruptly, and I slammed into her. "Oh, we need to discuss that. About me going to work tomorrow," she said.

I cupped the nape of her neck in one palm and pulled her close for a kiss. "Later, my love, later. Now, we have more important issues to discuss." I pressed my lips to hers and felt her relax against me. Her mouth opened, and I tasted what she had tasted, trying to discern which sweetness was her and which the salad dressing. I finally concluded it was all her as I plundered her mouth. Her knees weakened, and I tightened my grip. My lips curved in a small smile of accomplishment. I wanted her to trust me to hold her, to love her.

Later, on the bed, I encouraged her to trust me again as I stretched our lovemaking into a marathon of memorable delight. I undressed her slowly, in stages, laying my lips and hands on every new part of skin revealed. I felt gluttonous and almost guilty to be allowed once again to savor the taste, scent and touch of this beautiful feast. I found myself mindlessly muttering gratitude in my native tongue. She quivered beneath my fingers as I floated them across her soft flesh.

"I love how you love me," she whispered as she swept her

hair to one side so that I could press my lips to the side of her neck.

I slid out of my clothing and into her arms. I pulled her close, inserting my thigh between hers and finding the most delicious moist heat there. I sighed with contentment just as a huge weight dipped the mattress behind me. I stilled, trying to reorient myself so I would know what had occurred. Soft paws against my hip let me know that Julio had arrived. He hefted his considerable weight atop me and settled on my hip and outer thigh, wrapping his tail around his legs like any privileged temple cat.

"What's wrong?" Ella asked in a breathless voice. She opened her eyes and raised her head. "Oh," she said. "Oh, my."

He extended his claws, lightly kneading my flesh. I gasped in pain. "Can...can you get him off?" I asked quietly.

"Not without...hurting you, I don't think," she whispered worriedly.

"Ah, shit." I groaned and shuddered. Talk about a mood killer! "We have to try," I said.

Ella scooted off the bed and hurried around to my side. "Come on, big boy," she said, leaning to lift the cat in one smooth movement. I breathed out in relief and turned to see her scooting him out the door and shutting it firmly behind him. He meowed once in protest. I flipped over and propped on an elbow to admire Ella's luscious nakedness.

"You are so beautiful," I told her.

Her face colored as if in embarrassment, and she sped around to crawl under the blankets on her side. She pulled them so forcefully that she almost dumped me onto the floor.

Laughing, I rose and joined her between the sheets. "Now, where were we?" I asked.

She moved close and pressed her lips to mine. "Here. Right here," she muttered.

CHAPTER TWENTY-EIGHT

Ella

I had fallen asleep in Maddie's arms. I was fast coming to love the feel of her lean form against my naked body, even when just sleeping. She was so well carved by genetics, and a part of me envied that. Yet I was happy enough to enjoy it vicariously as we cuddled in the afterglow of lovemaking.

She woke me just after midnight. Because I was still naked, I had a sudden chill as she lifted then tucked the blankets snugly back around my body.

"What's happenin'?" I muttered, more asleep than awake.

"I have to go, sweetheart. There's been a car accident outside town, and Lizzie Horten went into labor. She's one of my patients."

"But...but Dr Mikas—"

"No, baby, he's gone home. You just go back to sleep. I'll be back as quickly as I can." She pressed her lips to my forehead, and I smiled.

I rolled onto my other side, easily reclaimed by sleep once again.

When I next woke, Julio was kissing me on the nose and forehead and sunlight was shining brightly through the window sheers.

"I thought we kicked you out of here," I grumbled as I rolled and checked the clock—and realized that I was running late for work. If I was, indeed, going in. Habit was hard to break. Also, Maddie and I hadn't discussed it enough to come to a firm decision the past night.

I checked the house as I brewed a single pod of coffee, but there was no sign that Maddie had returned. Her bag was moved somewhat, but it was probably from dressing during the night.

I fed Julio his morning kibble and then rushed into the shower. I hurried through, even though reliving the ecstasy of the previous night made me heavily distracted. When dry, I drew a huge heart in the steamy mirror using an old pink lipstick I had, hoping Maddie would see it that evening and be touched by the romantic gesture.

After getting dressed, I slung my handbag over my shoulder, grabbed up my phone and kissed Julio goodbye. I checked my phone on the way to my car, just to see if Maddie had called. I was surprised to see three calls from Sandy, calls I had no doubt missed while in the shower. I dialed and put it on speakerphone as I backed out of my parking space.

"Hello!" Sandy barked into the phone.

"Sandy, it's me, Ella. Everything okay? I know I'm running late, and I'm sorry—"

"Oh, honey. You've got to get over here right away." She began sobbing, and a band of steel constricted around my heart.

"S-Sandy? What's happened?"

"It's the doctor, Doc Maddie. It blew up and damn near killed her."

Something had blown up? Shock caused me to drift into the oncoming lane, and I barely missed colliding with a low-riding Mercury Cougar filled with smoking teens. They laid on the horn and shouted disparaging remarks as I righted my car and pulled it onto the shoulder.

"Ella? What was that noise? Where are you?"

"I—I'm on the road. Are you at the office?" I could barely whisper the question. Tears welled and spilled hot and brutal onto my cheeks.

"At the hospital. We're still in emergency." She sobbed loudly, and it hurt so badly that I pressed the disconnect button. I sat very still for a long moment. I was afraid to go to my Maddie. I was afraid of what I might find, the way you were afraid to go to the doctor when you found an odd lump residing in your breast.

Go to the doctor. I needed to go to the doctor.

I felt insane. I could feel pure insanity creeping up on me, making ready to tap me on the shoulder. And anger was a huge part of that insanity.

"Could you do that, God?" I whispered. "Could you be so cruel, so unjust?"

I shook my head and swiped at my tears with both hands. Maddie needed me. I needed to go to her. I needed to know.

After checking traffic, I floored the gas pedal, leaving a stream of honking horns and flying gravel behind me.

PART TWO

CHAPTER TWENTY-NINE

Maddie

The accident was bad. It looked as though a tractor-trailer had slammed into Lizzie and Darwin Horten's small Honda Accord. I slowed in my approach, wondering how such a crash could have occurred. It didn't make sense logistically, unless one driver had run a stop sign. The night sky was vivid with the flashing blue, white and red lights from the many police and rescue vehicles so it was hard to see details. I parked my SUV to one side and grabbed my battered medical valise from the back cargo area.

"What happened?" I queried as I approached Vance Blackwell, Sheriff of Estes County. He was a small man, unusual for a sheriff, I supposed, but he was scrappy and highly intelligent. His sharp eyes missed nothing. I'd worked with him on more than a dozen occasions and always left our encounters amazed by his acuity.

"Ahh, hell, Maddie. A long-haul driver fell asleep. There's a truck stop just east of us in Baldwin, and they still push on trying to get into Mississippi before they rest. Stupid! Stupid!" He spit onto the asphalt and shook his head.

"Is the driver okay?" I asked, covering my eyes and trying to see into the center of the accident.

"Yep, right as rain. Lizzie's done gone into labor, though, that's why we called you in. She won't make it to the hospital. She's pinned in somehow, so you probably have to deliver her here."

He'd started walking, and I tried to keep up. Who would think such short, skinny legs could move so quickly?

"Here she is, Doc. Rescue just arrived, but they ain't been able to get her out, and she says the baby's coming." He led me through the mass of rescue personnel right to the twisted, accordioned Accord. I heard Lizzie moan, and I bent to peer into the driver's side of the wreckage.

"Well, hell, Lizzie. You know I'm still gonna charge you for an office visit. You can't get out of paying by having that baby this way."

The joke had the desired effect. Her eyes lost their glazed sheen of fear and focused finally on my face.

"I'm really glad to see you, Doc," she gasped. "This boy says he's coming right now, and I just can't do much about it."

I knelt and realized with dismay that she was wearing jeans. I sighed. "How close are they, hon?" I patted her knee.

She moaned and I waited, head bowed. This low to the ground, I was almost asphyxiated by the heavy, oily smell of gas. Alarm jangled along my nerves. This was not the place we wanted to deliver a baby.

"Lizzie? What's holding you in the car? Can you see?" I studied the seat and the steering wheel, trying to figure out how to extricate her. I didn't see anything holding her, although she'd have to squeeze through the very narrow space between the broken seat and the steering wheel.

"Jaws of Life is on its way. Idiot Charles got the wrong truck. He and Allen have gone to get it," Vance said from behind me.

"I don't know, Doctor Maddie. They cut the seat belt but it didn't...oh!" She grimaced as another contraction shook her.

"Hang in there, Lizzie. No pushing, if you can help it."

I rose to my feet, dusted off my knees and pulled Vance aside.

"Do you smell that?" I whispered urgently. "Is gas leaking somewhere?"

He looked worried. "Yeah, I smell it. The truck driver is underneath his rig, checking the fuel tank. I don't know about the sedan, though it seems just as strong over there." He scrubbed a palm across his forehead, mussing his thick hair.

"We've got to get her out of there. Can you get one of the firemen to go around the passenger side and see what's holding her?"

Vance strode off, and I heard him barking orders.

"Hey there, Darwin," I said. Lizzie's husband was kneeling next the car, comforting his wife.

"I tol' her she shouldn't be drivin', Doctor. I offered to, I really did." He was in a panic. I patted his arm.

"I'm sure you did, Darwin. Now, let's just focus on getting your new baby boy here." I motioned him to the side, and I gently probed Lizzie's legs, which were still in the front box, near the car's pedals.

"Can you turn?" I asked, gently pulling her legs toward me. "Don't twist, though, just slide around."

Lizzie screamed, and I let go immediately, raising my hands. She fell silent and gasped loudly on each indrawn breath. "Something…somethin' pulled, Doc. I dunno…somethin' in my chest."

Broken ribs, I thought. I sat back on my haunches, wondering what to do next. There was no way she could deliver the baby naturally now. It would have to be a cesarean. Unfortunately, there was no way I could get a good vantage point to do the emergency surgery. There just wasn't room.

I got to my feet and moved to the passenger side. A young man in full fire gear was examining the floorboard. He saw me and backed out. "I can't see anything holding her," he said. "The seat is jammed, though, twisted around up pretty close to the wheel. I think that may be the issue."

I thanked him and then took his place in the passenger seat. Lizzie turned frightened eyes to me. "Doc, what are we gonna do?" she asked.

I pulled my stethoscope out of my pocket and listened to her chest. Yep, diminishing breath sounds. I laid a palm against her dark cheek as I listened, hoping to provide some ease.

"Lizzie. Lizzie, look here, hon." I snapped my fingers, as she seemed to be going into shock. "This is the situation. The Jaws of Life are coming, and I need you to not, *absolutely not*, have this baby. I think you've got some busted ribs, and we're gonna have to do surgery to get this newest little Horten out of you."

She cupped both hands in front of her groin. "I dunno, Doc. I'll try. Hurts somethin' fierce, though." She coughed and seemed almost to pass out from the pain. I backed out of the car, stood and scanned the scene. Most of the rescue personnel were standing around fidgeting but helpless. They looked at me with hope in their eyes, expectantly.

"Get a gurney ready," I called out. "Put it on this side. There's more maneuvering room, and I think it's our best bet when the Jaws free her. Darwin, hand me my bag!"

I knew how much pain removing her from the car was going to cause her, but I didn't want to start an IV for several reasons, not least of which was the added task of maneuvering a field IV out of the car along with her. Just getting Lizzie out would be task enough. I tangled my fingers in my bound hair in frustration.

Shit! Shit! Shit, I screamed inwardly. I just hoped that the extraction would go quickly, with no further delays.

New lights swept across the car, and I saw the rescue unit pull in. This one probably had the Jaws in it. I busied myself with preparing the IV and a minimal shot of morphine to help her pain ease after she was freed. After everything was prepared, I leaned into the car again and felt Lizzie's fast pulse. I smoothed her hair, gently scratching the scalp in between her short dreads. She was moaning and rocking her head back and forth.

Two firemen ran up with what looked like a pair of channellock pliers on steroids. "What's the status, Doc?" one asked.

"She needs out of there yesterday," I said.

The second man was examining the wreck, and then he and Darwin started discussing possibilities. The third man joined in, and I gnashed my teeth in frustration.

"Look, just take off the roof, will you? Do something. Hurry!"

The first fireman turned to me. "We're going to shear off the steering column along with this support here. Can you pull her that way when it's off?"

I nodded and motioned Darwin to my side. "We're gonna pull her this way when the steering wheel's off, but we have to be careful. Her ribs are broken, so try to keep her arms by her sides. We'll need to lift her to that gurney there, so I can assess her situation. Be prepared though, Darwin. You gotta be strong, because she's gonna scream like we're ripping her apart, okay?"

I watched his sweat- and tear-sheened face and noted the terror there. He tried to become strong, though, and I watched that battle with satisfaction, even as a grinding roar of torn metal made me wince.

I saw the light before I felt it. I was just reaching down to see if she'd been freed.

Then there was nothing.

CHAPTER THIRTY

Ella

The Estes Baptist Hospital might have been small but the entrances were still as confusing as all get out. I had parked in emergency parking but ended up having to race around to the side emergency door. Several people were crowding around the intake desk, and I stepped impatiently from foot to foot as I scowled at their backs.

After they left, I started to ask after Maddie but had a moment of clarity. "Is Sandy Webber nearby? She asked me to come here."

The receptionist looked me over disdainfully. "Sandy? Where do you know her from?"

I gritted my teeth and then forced them to relax. "We work together—at Dr Salas's office."

Her face fell and new terror gripped me. "Alex, take her on back to where Sandy is. In waiting room two," she told the young man next to her.

He immediately left the triage area and pressed the button that opened the heavy double doors that led into emergency.

"So you work with Doctor Maddie?" he asked as I breathlessly tried to keep up with him.

"I do," I said. "For most of a year now."

He shook his head and a lifeless lock of dark hair bobbed against his forehead. "It's just awful, what happened. She's a hero, though, no doubt about that."

I was just going to press for more details, but a copiously weeping Sandy, who draped herself in my arms, waylaid me. I nodded my thanks to Alex and guided Sandy to a chair in the crowded waiting room. I saw Sheriff Blackwell, who was smudged with soot and looked like he'd had an awful night. Several firemen were there too, one with a wounded, bandaged arm laying on his chest. I turned my attention back to Sandy and held her by her upper arms so she would look at me.

"Sandy, where is Maddie? What happened to her?"

She just shook her head and blubbered on. I let go of her and straightened. I was numb and could not gather my thoughts together to know how to proceed.

"They took her down for an MRI," Vance said as he approached us.

"Mama?"

A thirty-something woman, blond hair in a low side ponytail, entered the room and made a beeline for Sandy. She carried two cups of coffee, placed them on an end table and sat to pull Sandy into a close embrace.

"Shh, Mama. It's going to be all right. You know it is. Real bad things never happen to truly good people. God looks after them. Doc Maddie is gonna be okay, you just wait and see." She jostled Sandy gently. "Now, Mama, come on. Don't take on so."

She noticed me suddenly and stuck out her hand. "You must be Ella. I'm Cynthia, Sandy's girl. It's good to meet you, just the worst of circumstances, though."

I took her hand and murmured pleasantries. "So, what exactly happened?" I asked the room in general.

Sandy straightened and blotted her face with a tissue. "She was out on Gulfstream, right there offa I-10—"

"A trucker fell asleep at the wheel," Vance interjected. "He T-boned Darwin Horten's car as it was turning off I-10 onto Gulfstream. Lizzie, you know Lizzie, well, she was driving and got trapped behind the steering wheel somehow."

"She's pregnant...was pregnant," Sandy said as she burst into a fresh bout of sobbing.

"Doc Maddie and the rescue boys were trying to get her out when all of a sudden gas fumes ignited. It musta been gathering fumes under the Horten car. We were checking the truck tank, but the explosion came out from under the car."

"You. You mean it exploded? But where was...Doctor Maddie?" I studied his face, with eyes that I knew had to be wide and terrified. I was trying so very hard to keep myself together.

Vance didn't say anything right away, just fiddled with his belt buckle with both hands. Finally, he dropped those hands apologetically. "She was...ah...right next to the car. She was thrown free but landed hard against the cinderblock wall of Lou's Stop and Shop, then fell onto the asphalt. She's...well, she's banged up pretty badly but they're mostly worried about her brain. He called it a traumatic brain injury and..."

"They say there may be swelling," Sandy added dully, speaking into a tissue as she rocked back and forth, as if soothing herself. "They are scanning her now to see if they have to operate to relieve the pressure. They're not sure of how bad the damage is otherwise."

My knees gave, and I tumbled to the floor, eased down by Vance's grasp. I was sure I lost consciousness; I eventually came back to my senses, hearing Sandy calling my name. She and her daughter, Cynthia, were hovering over me, seeming to be truly concerned. I agonized that I couldn't tell anyone what my Maddie meant to me. All I could do was weep, curled into a fetal curve onto the hard, stained carpet of that waiting room floor.

CHAPTER THIRTY-ONE

Maddie

I imagined I was back in the womb, and I perplexed myself by wondering how I could have such cognition while wrapped in the soft, warm fluid of my mother's body. Surely infants weren't self-aware before birth. The leading literatures said that came much later, if I remembered correctly, at about fifteen to twenty months. I shifted one hand, to touch the walls of the uterus, but pain rebounded throughout my entire body, finally stopping to set up a home in my head. It throbbed and my hands formed into claws. I wanted to rip off my head, but the effort just seemed to be too much. I drifted, rolling into each throb as it happened, riding them just so I could bear the pain.

I thought it was another time. The throbbing had stopped, finally, and I took in a deep breath.

"Don't move, sweetie," a kind, female voice said next to me. "This shouldn't take long. We just want to see what's going on in that pretty head of yours."

I lurched forward on some kind of hard bed, and the movement sent what felt like shards of glass throughout my entire body. I moaned and crawled toward complete consciousness but found a locked steel door blocking me. I wasn't sure whether it was in my mind or real. Loud knocking surrounded me, and I screamed aloud. The effort made my whole body spasm, and I went dark again.

The next time I opened my eyes, I saw only darkness. For a moment, I thought I had lost my vision, but then pale shadows emerged from the darkness. A fuzziness persisted in front of my eyes and I blinked them to clear it away. It didn't work.

I remembered visiting *Mama* with my *mami*. She was speaking to me, but I couldn't understand her. The subtle movements of her mouth were familiar, and when *Papa* spoke to her, I realized it was Spanish. Of course, I thought with some amusement. The heavy, wet air meant I was in Puerto Rico. I could hear the amazingly loud chirping calls of the *coqui*, the tiny green frogs snug in their tree nests as they called for lovers to come for conjugal visits.

My cousin, Paco, threw the ball at me, and it was so heavy that it knocked me to the dirt and gravel street in front of my grandmother's house. A rock split my thigh, and the pain shot along my nerves like a scorching brand.

"*Mama!*" I cried out. My grandmother left the porch and lifted me, all the while scolding Paco. She told him he was too big, bigger than me, and he needed to take care—*cuidado, cuidado.*

My neck was throbbing, harder than the worst headache I'd ever had. I whimpered, and I was in class. It was Foster's Prep, in Manhattan. I'd caught the eye of Darla Wright Johns, one of the prettiest girls in our school. She was smart too and—God, I would never be smart again. I wept, and it made my head throb as hard as my neck. My back ached.

"Don't do that, Paco. *Cuidado.* Mama says *cuidado*," I muttered.

"What did you say?" someone asked. The voice was familiar, yet not.

"*Mami?* Are you there, *Mami?* Paco hurt me, and *Mama* says—"

"Maddie?"

"Corinthia Salas! You march back up there, right now, and apologize to your father. I will not have a daughter of mine speak to an adult in such a manner. *Dios Mio! Ahora, dile lo sientes.*"

"*Papi. Lo siento, Papi.*" I wept and buried my face in his shoulder. He patted my back and cold fingers held my hand. They weren't his short, stubby fingers, but long, slender ones.

"A woman," I muttered. "Who is that woman?"

The smell of rubbing alcohol inundated me, and I remembered being in medical school. Texas women were a different breed, not like women anywhere else in the United States. At least none of the states I'd been in. I'd been a little afraid of them, intimidated by their overt assertiveness.

Cold touched my arm, and the pain left me. I balled up my fist and felt no throb resulting from the movement. My fist slammed hard to one side and connected forcefully with something. It was soft and fortunately didn't cause more pain.

I kissed Darla one day, after what passed as our fitness hour. Her lips were chapped from the December winds, and they felt rough beneath mine. She had asked for the kiss, but I had hesitated. Suppose it was a prank meant to embarrass me? Could I trust her? I heard footsteps behind me, and we both turned to find the very formidable Mrs. Anthony, of the Greek classics class, approaching us. We broke apart and scattered in two different directions.

"I wet my pants," I whispered. "I'm so sorry."

"It's okay, Dr Salas. You're catheterized," someone said and patted my hand. I smelled Heavensent perfume. My *mami* didn't wear that. She wore Chanel. Was I a doctor?

"Doctor, doctor, doctor," I said, trying on the word. It sounded nice but didn't fit.

I heard people talking in hushed tones, but there were weighty strings laying across my lips, several thick ones, and I brought a hand up to brush them away. I hit sharp edges instead, and something crashed loudly. It made my head throb once again, and I whimpered and moaned.

"Make it stop, can't you make it stop, *Mami*? I won't be rude to *Papi*. The rice was not really burnt, though, just so you know."

A welcome, comforting heat washed across me. Then I was back in my mother's womb, and the pain faded into the background. I began to sing. My grandmother sang this song to me when I was a baby.

"But wait," I told her. "I'm not born yet. Wait until I am born. Then you can sing to me, and I can sing it with you. Here no one can hear me."

I wept, wanting to be heard.

CHAPTER THIRTY-TWO

Ella

My first sight of Maddie after the accident caused my heart to clench in my chest and my eyes, which I had thought completely cried out, to well up again. Sandy and I clung together like two castaways in an ocean devoid of land.

"Oh, God, she looks awful," Sandy said quietly. "Do you think she'll ever be okay?"

I sighed deeply. "She has to, Sandy. It's like Cynthia said, she's good people."

My insanity had stepped aside for a while, allowing me to focus on the here and now. I assessed Maddie with a medical eye.

She was banged up, no doubt about it. Her right eye was bright red and swollen shut, her bottom lip split. Her right arm was splinted, and there was a cage under her blankets; no doubt her legs were bruised, maybe even abraded from the asphalt. The little finger on her left hand was splinted, so it was probably broken as well. I could not even imagine the level of pain she was experiencing.

A nurse strode rapidly into the room and hung a new IV bag. She smiled and nodded at us. "Y'all can come close, but I think it'll be some time before she comes back to herself. We think her head was banged pretty hard." She paused and looked down at Maddie. "Poor little thing," she added. "You know, my granddaddy goes to see her, has been since she took over for Dr Pembroke. I just hate that this has happened to her."

I let Sandy go and moved closer to the bed. I wanted so badly to touch her that my hands shook. "Me too," I agreed softly.

"I know she looks a sight, all swollen and all, but you'd be surprised how the body can heal itself. You two need anything just let me know." She turned to go but turned back. "Don't try to move her or even wake her up. She needs to rest now, more than anything."

"Sandy, what happened out there?" I asked a short time later. I was blinking back tears but managing to keep my face immobile as stone. I couldn't let Sandy see how I really felt about Maddie. Breaking down in the waiting room had been more than enough exposure.

Sandy was studying the monitoring machines. "Gas fumes can be lit really easy. It doesn't take much."

"Why didn't the rescue guys clear the area? I mean, isn't that standard procedure?" I couldn't help the sharp tone that invaded my voice.

She looked up at me. "You heard Vance. She was trying to deliver Lizzie, but they couldn't get her out of the car."

I looked down at Maddie's bandaged, tubing-pierced hands and suddenly flashed back to those hands moving on and in my body. I closed my eyes, wanting very badly to feel that again. I vowed then and there that I would again. Whatever it took, I would bring Maddie back to me. I trembled inside, fear overtaking me. What if...? No, I couldn't think that way. Maddie was my love. It had taken me so long to find her...

"Oh, no," Sandy said and I swiveled my head to gape at her. "What?"

"Her aunt lives just west of town. We need to let her know, but I'm not sure how to contact her. I can't even remember her name." Sandy's face wore panic. I had to put her mind at ease.

"What about those contact forms we keep at the office? The ones that we all fill out for our human resources files. Did she do one?" I looked back at Maddie, and my hands twitched, wanting to touch her. Actually, I wanted to wake her and have her smile that adorable smile at me.

"Ella, you are a lifesaver. I'm going to run over there and see if I can find it. If I do, I'll call her aunt. Will you be okay here? They're gonna run us out of here soon so they can do the next meal, though I don't suppose she'll get one. The cafeteria's on the second floor, if you want to duck out then come and stay here at the hospital a little longer."

I turned to her. "Thank you, Sandy. I…I'm sorry about earlier. It's just such a shock."

She took one of my hands in hers and patted it repeatedly. "That's perfectly all right, sweetie. It's hit us all hard. You just never think something like this will happen to someone you… you know."

A sob shook her, and I drew her into my arms. "Let's focus on the most important stuff and we'll get through this," I said in my calmest voice. "While you're at the office, why don't you pick up the day list sheet for today? We'll need to call and cancel with everyone."

She grabbed up her leather pocketbook from the chair, suddenly filled with purpose. "Oh, heck yeah. I also need to see if I can find another doctor close by who can fill in for her. You know, just till she gets back on her feet." She glanced nervously at the bed. "Well, I'll go. If she wakes up…well, you tell her Sandy says hey, will you do that?"

"Of course I will, Sandy. Now, scoot on. I bet you have a line of early patients waiting for you already." I made a shooing motion toward the door.

Alone with Maddie, I could finally relax my shoulders. I felt like a tulip after the first frigid frost of fall. My body—my stem—had weakened, and I wasn't sure I could remain upright any longer. I dragged the chair closer to the bed and sat, my hand stroking Maddie's unsplinted arm. I wondered if she could feel me, if she knew I was near.

"Maddie? Maddie, honey. I'm here. Come back to me, my darling. Do you remember the conference?" I smiled and pressed my forehead to her forearm, stilling my hands. "The fun we had skating? My legs still hurt."

How stupid was that? I thought, to talk about my minor pain when the agony that she must be... I shook my head. I needed food and more coffee if I was going to be with her.

"Maddie? Honey, I need to go downstairs for just a minute. But I'll be back, I promise." I sobbed suddenly and unexpectedly, and my cheeks warmed with hot, fresh tears. "Damn it," I muttered. I mopped at my eyes with my sleeve. "Okay. I'm going but not for long. Just for coffee. I'll tell them at the nurses' station so you won't be alone, okay?"

I moved to the door, walking backward, watching her, willing her to smile and respond. There was no movement. It was like my Maddie had gone away.

CHAPTER THIRTY-THREE

Maddie

People surrounded me. They were talking, but I couldn't understand them. The words pounding against my eardrums hurt very badly, however, and I wanted to tell them to talk more quietly. To my horror, I realized I couldn't tell them. The words wouldn't come to me. I could think them but only briefly before they drifted away. Also, the strings still lay across and in my mouth, stitching it closed, and my tongue lay limp and useless inside my mouth.

"Do you think she hears us?" a voice asked.

I was excited that I understood. But who was that? I knew that voice. It saddened me that it wasn't my mother, and I sobbed helplessly. I wasn't prone to tears, so my reaction confused and horrified me. But only momentarily. My thoughts followed the idea of my mother, and I saw her walking away. As she walked, she visibly aged until she crumbled into dust right before my eyes.

"*Mami!*" I screamed, but I thought it was only in my mind. I raced after her. My hands reached out, but they only brushed her shirt before she disintegrated completely. My heart felt as though it had torn in two. I had lost everything that meant anything to me.

"Time to go back, *mi corazon*. It is not your time yet," my mother whispered. Her face appeared before me. I fell into her deep brown eyes, pillowing my head on the creases that surrounded those eyes. Laugh lines, I thought.

A woman comforted me by patting my hand. I didn't know her, but I admired her deep green eyes and thick blond hair. She was crying, as well.

"Was she your mother too?" I asked in my mind. "Are you my sister? I never had a sister."

A larger woman drew me into her arms. She smelled familiar, but her words were in English, and I couldn't grasp what she was saying. I pulled back and looked at her with one eye. The other eye wouldn't work, for some odd reason. She wasn't my mother either, and I wept anew. I was two years old, alone in a cold, teetering world, and I wanted the security of my mother, or at the very least, my grandmother.

I fell into a deep hole and serenely pulled it in after me.

I woke at night. My arm was throbbing, and I tried to lift it. It was too heavy, so I raised my head to see what was wrong. The entire arm appeared stark white in the dimness. I realized that I was in a hospital bed. A nasal cannula was forcing frigid oxygen into my nose, and my throat felt raw from it. Or had I been screaming? I really didn't know.

I tried to think about why I would be in a hospital but nothing would come to me. I had spent many years sleeping in hospitals, but this felt different. Residency. Yes, I was a physician. I shifted tentatively and then had to grit my teeth as pain rocketed through my entire body. I'd been hurt somehow.

Abrupt, acute nausea washed across me. Despite the pain caused by the movement, I leaned to one side and retched repeatedly. Sudden alarms shrieked all around me, and I screamed out as the sounds attacked my ears. My less encumbered hand lifted to cover my ears.

Bright light blinded me as someone switched it on, and I felt my body begin to seize up, I was bending backward against my will, my muscles contracting severely.

People surrounded me. My body was relaxed again, but there was still some nausea and I felt like the room was spinning. I cracked the lids of my good eye and saw dim figures standing next to my bed. Some were scurrying around very busily; others stood sentinel. There was something in my mouth and throat. I realized with some alarm that I was intubated. This meant I needed help to breathe. Tears welled again and spilled down my cheeks. My nose felt like a huge apple sitting in the middle of my face, and that damned headache was back. My hearing was hypersensitive, and each squeak of a nurse's shoes made me quake inside. Luckily, those caring for me knew to speak softly.

I calmed and tried to take stock of my situation, trying desperately to remember what had happened to me. What incident had brought me to this place? Maybe I had been in a car accident. If so, I didn't remember it at all. It was like I was in a box. My memory could go so far one way, so far another. Beyond those walls, there was nothing.

I schooled myself to take one moment at a time. I felt as though I had studied Zen Buddhism at some point, and it seemed to fit. Seemed to be what I needed most at this point.

I felt drugged suddenly, dopey. I looked at the faces around me and saw that they were all strangers. That made me sad, very sad. I needed to be with people who cared for me, not all these strangers.

"Go away!" I cried, sweeping one arm out to banish all of them. I paused in midsweep. "Go away," I said again, much softer. Horror filled me. I could not understand the words I was saying. They sounded all wrong.

CHAPTER THIRTY-FOUR

Ella

Dr Stephen Dorsey came into Maddie's room carrying a lightweight plastic folding chair and Maddie's chart. He unfolded the chair with some aplomb and placed it next to the two chairs already at the foot of Maddie's bed. He motioned for us to sit in them as he took a seat on the plastic chair and crossed his legs. After Maddie's Aunt Florida and I were seated, he opened up Maddie's chart and took in a deep breath.

"Well. Dr Salas was in a terrible accident. She was lucky in a lot of ways. Many gas explosions lead to fires and horrible burns when the gas ignites. She experienced none of that. She was, however, thrown away from the car with some force and sustained a few broken bones."

He flipped a page and studied it. I studied his intelligent thirty-something face. He was handsome but seemed studious.

"Broken bones will heal, of course. What we are concerned with the most is an area of edema, or swelling, on the right side of Dr Salas's brain. Though it's significant, we opted not to do surgery. Instead, we have increased her oxygen and lowered her body temperature to allow her body to process this fluid. Her neurologist, Amelia Penn, seems to think this is the best course of treatment in this particular case. Well, that and certain medications that she has prescribed."

He paused to study each of us as he adjusted his glasses. "So, now let's talk about the future."

He looked directly at me. "Mrs. Salas here has said that I can talk freely in front of you. Is this all right with you?"

I nodded, and he continued.

"Whenever you have this kind of injury, which is a closed brain injury, one also sees a contrecoup injury. This means the brain bounced around in her head, which injured it in a specific way, from the contusion on both sides of her brain. We don't think there's a lot of axonal twisting, which often does happen in these kinds of accidents, but there is certainly concussion, and this may lead us to something called postconcussive disorder."

He uncrossed his legs and leaned closer to us. "This disorder could manifest in a myriad of different ways. There could be minor changes, but in this situation, I think they may be significant and go on for some time—"

A tiny gasp escaped me, and I felt a sob welling in my throat. "Will she recover, Dr Dorsey?"

He sighed. "Yes, to some extent, but no, not completely."

I covered my mouth with one hand. I had to stuff down that sob, that scream that wanted to get loose.

"She's relatively young, and her natural high level of intelligence will help her brain create new neural pathways, allowing her to do just about everything she did before, just slightly differently. Well, almost everything. But there's also the issue of her tolerance and energy level. This kind of injury can manifest in anger and intolerance to even the smallest irritant, so don't be surprised by her anger and frustration. It's a given that there will be some of that. The brain is an intricate organ, and injuries to it can cause all manner of emotional and intellectual misfiring."

He paused and fingered his clean-shaven chin. "Life will be very different for her, and she will need long-term continued care and therapy. In injuries like this, the motion inside the skull can cause microtears of the brain matter. This will, no doubt, cause scarring in the brain which might lead to an ataxic, or drunken-like gait, or even aphasia, which are problems with speech, depending on where the scarring is. That's something that medicine just can't fix."

Silence fell in the room, the only sound the mild beeping and whooshing of the various machines connected to Maddie.

"So, any questions?" he asked.

"Why is she hooked up to the breathing machine?" Florida asked. "Is she not able to breathe on her own?"

"She had a bad spell a while back, and we decided that getting as much oxygen in her as we could would help her," he explained. "She kept pulling out the cannula, that tubing that was giving her extra oxygen. She'll come off the machine soon, we hope. We have her sedated until that happens."

Florida nodded and shifted restlessly in her chair.

I was thinking how important being a doctor was to Maddie. "She won't be able to practice medicine anymore, will she?" I asked sadly. "She'll hate that."

He sighed and thoughtfully patted Maddie's chart against his knee. "Let's not get that far ahead. I don't want any of us to be too negative. Although the scans show that the swelling and bruising is pretty severe, she may rebound better than any of us believe after therapy. We're in a wait-and-see mode. Dr Penn says that she has seen eventual complete recoveries after an injury like this. Sometimes people only have mild stammers or gait issues, but all their cognition comes back. Some are physically fine, but they lose all short-term memory. So, as you can see, I really can't answer that question just yet. Anything else?"

We both shook our heads, and he stood and folded his chair. "You can ask for me at the nurses' station if you think of anything else. My advice is just to be here for her and be very, very grateful that she is alive."

We sat, lost in thought, after Dr Dorsey left the room. I watched the slow rise and fall of Maddie's chest as the machine hissed. I felt oddly empty inside. It was as though I had no emotion left—for anything.

Florida patted my hand as she stood. I really had come to like Maddie's aunt. She was a comfortable, down-to-earth woman and had been unusually consoling to me. I found myself wondering if she knew about Maddie and me. How could that be, though, unless Maddie had called her?

"I guess we'd better get to the church. We only have about twenty minutes to get there," she said. She moved to the bed and pressed a kiss to Maddie's forehead. "Fight your way back, little Corinthia," she whispered.

"I'll wait for you in the hall," she told me as she passed by toward the door.

I was grateful for the time alone with Maddie. I took her hand and caressed it as I leaned to press my cheek to the less wounded side of her face. "I love you, Maddie, darling. I promise I'll be back soon."

There was, of course, no response.

The funeral was beautiful, if such an event could be called that. The saddest part was the tiny white coffin for the baby who'd never been officially born before dying. The Horten and Collins families had decided to combine Lizzie, Darwin and the baby boy's funeral into one service. I thought that was a good idea.

Sandy, of course, was devastated, sobbing uncontrollably and barely able to stand. She had known Lizzie longer than I had and had followed her pregnancy closely. She also knew Lizzie's husband, Darwin, who I'd never met before.

The firefighter's funeral had been two days ago. Florida, Sandy and I had attended that one as well. I felt as though I attended all these for Maddie. She would have been there if she could have been, and she would want to know all about them as soon as she got better.

CHAPTER THIRTY-FIVE

Maddie

I woke into grayness. Sudden terror filled me. I couldn't swallow or move my head. A sort of claustrophobia washed over me, but I worked hard to calm myself, realizing that a machine was breathing for me. I held my breath until the machine caught up with the breaths I felt I should be taking. I exhaled with the machine and counted each uptake the machine made for me: sixteen, then sixteen again. I was getting enough air. Then I had a new fear—suppose the machine failed and I suffocated. Only an act of steel will kept me from thrashing about, and I forced the failure thought from my mind. *Unreasonable*, I told myself, *remarkably unusual for the machines to fail.*

"Dr Salas! You're awake!" a young, small-statured nurse exclaimed as she entered the room. "I wondered what that strange reading out there was all about."

She studied my face, and I guessed she read calm there. "Just nod or shake your head, okay? Are you in any pain?"

I shook my head to one side in the negative.

"Good." She paused a long beat, still studying me. "Would you like the breathing tube out?"

Oh my God! I was ecstatic to discover that it didn't have to be permanent. I nodded as well as I was able.

She smiled. "Okay. I'm going to go check with Dr Dorsey and see what he says about it. Be right back."

When she left the room, I studied my surroundings. It was a typical hospital room. I recognized the dark ocean green used by the… Funny, I couldn't remember the name of the hospital. I had to still be in… Maypearl. Yes, Maypearl, Alabama. I worked there, as a physician.

"Well, well, Dr Salas. How are you feeling?" asked the doctor as he and the nurse entered my room.

Stupid man, I thought, even as I studied him. Medium height, athletic build, but nerdy with glasses and an unkempt shock of black hair. How did he expect me to respond?

His apologetic smile, filled with perfectly straight teeth, was genuine. "Well. That was a dumb question, huh? Let's get this tube out and we'll talk then," he said.

I gave him a weak thumbs-up with my less-injured hand, and he moved to the head of the bed. The process of the tube leaving my body, while welcome, was surely classified as one of the many torture devices of the Spanish Inquisition. It hurt but was completed quickly. I choked on the water the small nurse provided, and shards of pain resurfaced. I moaned and tried to curl on one side, but the pain in my legs and the many clear rubber tubes inserted into my body prevented it.

The doctor pulled a chair closer to the bed and sat in it. "Dr Salas, I'm Dr Dorsey. I doubt you remember what happened to you, but you were in a car that exploded several weeks ago. The explosion tossed you into the air and against a building. You have a concussion. You had some swelling, but that's gone down now. We did not operate but let time work in your favor."

The hospital was waking up around us. I could hear increased activity and voices out in the halls.

I shifted my position slightly, carefully, trying to avoid any more pain. "How long?" I asked.

I stopped in shock, puzzled. Was my hearing bad? No, my hearing was acutely aware. I looked at his face, which was frowning, and his eyes were concerned. Okay, something was wrong. I tried again.

"How long ago?" I asked, then pressed my lips together. I was aphasic. "No, no, no!" I cried out, and my words sounded like a crow cawing.

"Dr Salas," Dr Dorsey said as he grasped my shoulders. I was unaware of it, but I'd sat upright in the bed, and my cast-bound right arm was wildly slinging about. My left arm was pulling painfully against the IV tubing.

"Give just one of halo," Dorsey instructed the nurse.

Yes, calm me down, I thought. It was as though I was outside my body, tutting at myself for my improper antics. Within seconds, the drug had taken control, and I was able to stop spasming.

"Dr Salas," Dr Dorsey said calmly, looking directly into my eyes. "You need to stay calm. We will determine what's causing the aphasia. In the meantime, answer these questions for me by moving your head. Don't try to talk."

He released his hold on me and took a seat. "Now, in your opinion, how is your cognition? Do you understand everything I am saying?"

I nodded.

"Good. That's a positive sign." There was that nice smile again. "Do you remember the accident?"

I shook my head.

"That's not uncommon. I didn't really expect you to. This inability to talk may clear up after some more time has passed. We've kept you sedated for the past four weeks so that your brain could begin to heal."

I grew agitated again, and he laid a calming hand on my forearm. "Your patients are being looked after. Don't worry about that. Your only thoughts should be focused on your continued healing. It's going to take some time, but I promise we'll get you back home as quickly as we can, okay?"

I nodded but couldn't help the tear that spilled onto my cheek. Four weeks! That was crazy!

The doctor rose and shoved the chair back. "By the way, you had a greenstick on that right arm, but it's knitting very nicely. I think the cast can come off sometime this week, and we'll get you out of that bed and into some therapy." He grabbed my chart, studied me briefly and then hurried from the room.

The nurse approached and adjusted my tubing. She rearranged my arms on top of the sheet. "Are you warm enough, honey? We've been keeping the temp pretty low in here." She adjusted the oxygen at the head of the bed and positioned a nasal cannula. "We'll keep a little oxygen going for another day or two, okay?"

I realized suddenly that I was cold. "I'm cold," I said and watched her study me blankly.

"Let's not talk now, Dr Salas. Just indicate to me what you need. Is the oxygen okay?"

I nodded.

"But you're cold?" she asked.

I nodded.

"Well, then. I'm gonna march right out to the nurses' station and fetch you a cozy blanket from the warmer. I'll be right back."

After she left, I turned my head and looked past the monitoring machines and through the window to the growing daylight outside.

"Pretty," I said. The word sounded like an exotic disease.

CHAPTER THIRTY-SIX

Ella

Abby Hamilton died, finally succumbing to the cancer that had taken over her small body. When Sandy told me the news, I felt as though I couldn't breathe.

"How can we go to another funeral?" Sandy stated, her eyes red and rimmed with unshed tears. I pulled her close and hugged her as she allowed herself to weep.

We had grown close during the weeks that Maddie had been in the hospital. We often went together to see her after work, although I loved the late nights when I would sneak in alone and hold my dearest love's hand until I was sleepy enough to drive home and go to bed. Florida was there some evenings, and I think she came every morning as well.

"We'll do fine," I told Sandy. "We loved her, and we have to say goodbye properly."

Sandy nodded as Dr McLean came down the hall from Maddie's office. Randy McLean was a very nice, friendly man and a competent doctor. It wasn't his fault that he wasn't Maddie. Still, every time I saw him come from her office, I grew angry.

He patted Sandy on the shoulder. "Here's the death certificate. I called the funeral home before I left the house, but I didn't wait around for them. Do you think you can get this copy to them?"

Sandy scrubbed at her eyes and blew her nose loudly. "Absolutely, Dr McLean. Right away."

He went back into the office, and I lifted the next folder from the stack and stepped into the waiting room. "DunDun?" I called out.

DunDun Morris was a sweet, shy redhead being treated for recurring eczema. He nodded shyly as he passed me and stepped into the back hallway.

"Come this way, and we'll get you situated," I said as I led him along the hallway. "So the hydrocortisone cream didn't work for you?"

"No, ma'am. I think it gets washed off when I do the drying after the wash, even though I try to be careful. I've tried just about everything now." He was soft-spoken, and I had to listen closely to hear him. I knew he worked at Wheelie's Car Wash most days after school.

"Well, I'm sure Dr McLean will come up with a new treatment plan that will work better."

"Will Doctor Maddie be back soon?" he asked as I took his vitals. "I sure do miss her. We had a lot of fun just talking."

My hands trembled as I replaced the ear thermometer into its holder. I sighed.

"I don't really know, DunDun. The doctors over at the hospital are trying to wake her up, but she just doesn't seem to want to come out of it. Believe me, we miss her too."

The door opened, and Dr McLean came in followed by Sandy. She stayed behind the door and beckoned me out

"They think she's waking up!" she crowed in a loud whisper.

I blinked slowly. "For real?"

She nodded. "That's what Cassie said. I just got off the phone with her. Let's go call Florida, and we'll meet her there after work. This I gotta see for myself." She hurried off. I followed in a daze. Could Maddie really be coming back to us after all these weeks?

The hospital was winding down although the halls were still packed with visitors. Most of the nursing staff changed shifts at three, and by five thirty, the new night staff was in place and smoothly taking care of sorting the end-of-day medications and charting.

The three of us met outside and progressed to Maddie's room together. Now, outside her door, we paused and looked at one another. This would be a very great day if what Cassie had told us were true. We'd been depressed about Maddie's condition for long enough. We needed some good news.

She was sitting up when we entered the room. My heart thrilled upon seeing this. I rushed to her side. She raised her eyes and looked at me. Most of the bruises and cuts had healed, though there was still some discoloration around her right eye. She looked so beautiful, yet so frail. Her deep brown eyes seemed clouded, and I wondered if she saw me clearly.

"Lord, girl, you are a sight for sore eyes," Sandy said as she approached the opposite side of the bed. "You look really good considering what you've been through. Are you feeling okay?"

Maddie nodded but looked away from us, out the window. She seemed disinterested.

"Maddie?" I said. She turned back around. I saw no recognition in her eyes. "It's Ella. And this is Sandy. We work for you. Do you remember us?"

She looked from me to Sandy then back again. Nothing.

"Corinthia?"

Her head snapped around upon hearing this name, and she peered suspiciously at Florida. Maddie's lips moved, but no sound came out.

My heart began a frantic two-step in my chest. *It was still early*, I told myself. *The brain is still healing. She will remember us when it does.*

Why wasn't I convinced?

Florida moved closer and laid her hand on Maddie's cast. "It's *Tia* Florida, honey. We're going to get you home soon. It should only be a few more days and then you can come home to my house and we'll have you right as rain in no time. How does that sound?"

Maddie was listening intently, but she didn't speak. After some time, she lifted her other hand and placed it atop her aunt's. I desperately hoped that this was a good sign.

Sandy pulled me aside and whispered in my ear. "I'm gonna go see if I can find that sawbones and find out what's going on here."

"Sandy—" I wanted to reiterate to her what the doctor had explained to Florida and me a few weeks ago, but she was gone. I moved back to Maddie, determined to bring her out of this fugue state.

"Maddie, I want to let you know that everything at the office is just fine. Sandy found a new young doctor named Randolph McLean to do your office hours. He seems nice enough. He's not you, of course, but I don't think anyone's getting poor treatment."

Maddie nodded, so I knew she heard me, but she still seemed disinterested. She was studying Florida, head cocked to one side.

I remembered suddenly how she had looked at me in a similar way, and my heart actually ached. I couldn't catch my breath for a moment. I struggled to stifle the panic I felt.

Sandy bustled back into the room, drawing Maddie's attention.

"Maddie, honey, we'll be right back," Sandy said, smiling at her as she motioned Florida and me from the room.

"The doctor wants to see us at the nurse desk, just to talk about what's going on with Maddie," she told us once we were in the hallway.

She led the way through the intricate labyrinth where the nurses for the neurology ward were stationed. Flat monitors were mounted on one central wall, visible from all angles, and I felt glad that Maddie was so well looked after. Dr Dorsey stood by an alcove, reading papers that were in a folder. He heard us, snapped the folder shut and welcomed us with a smile. He escorted us through the alcove and into a small conference room, closing the door behind us.

"Ladies, if you all will have a seat, we can talk about Dr Salas's course of treatment." He took the remaining fourth chair and leaned back in it.

"Now, let me get this straight." He pointed at Florida. "You are her only family?"

"Yes." Florida nodded. "I'm her aunt. Her mother is still living but suffers from severe Alzheimer's."

"Ahh," he said, nodding sagely. "And you two work with her, in her medical practice?"

We nodded.

"I've been with Doctor Maddie since she took over for our previous Maypearl physician, Richard Pembroke," Sandy said.

Dr Dorsey nodded again and passed the folder to Florida. "Before we go any further with our discussion, I need you to sign this release, saying it is okay for the staff here to talk with Dr Salas's employees. I mean no disrespect, ladies," he said to Sandy and me. "It's all that legal mumbo jumbo that we have to take care of."

Florida signed the forms without hesitation, and Dr Dorsey began talking.

CHAPTER THIRTY-SEVEN

Maddie

Some days I sat in my bedroom and stared out the window, it being all I could do. I didn't much care for those days. I was sure at one point in my life, I'd been an energetic, even productive person. I was certainly well liked, as evidenced by the constant stream of visitors I had each week. Now, sitting on the side of my double bed in my tiny bedroom, I sighed. I turned and studied the board. It was Tuesday, November first, and the digital clock told me it was eight fifteen in the morning. I saw no appointments listed for today. I had nowhere to be. That was a huge relief. I could sit, by myself, and allow my mind to relax.

I stood and reached for my cane. I had picked out plain black, of course, but Ella had decorated it with colorful cat-face stickers all the way down. They didn't look like cats to me, but that was what she said they were. It was pretty.

I made my way into my bathroom. Studying my bathroom list, I began to follow it religiously. *Tia* had made it on a magnetic board, and I was to move a circle over every time I completed a task. I moved it from toilet to shower. I loved the shower. I often ran all the hot water out of the hot water tank, but *Tia* said it was okay. I undressed and then checked the list taped to the curtain.

In the beginning, right after I came home, I had washed my face and body so many times each morning, forgetting that I had already done it, that I made my skin raw and infected. Now, I could use the wax pencil and mark off everything that I washed, so I could remember and not do it again.

Another coping mechanism that Wendy Wagner, my therapist, had taught me was making sure that everything had a home. After I washed and dried my hair and body, I went to the sink and moved the lotion out of its home. I left it out there after I used it, and I did the same all the way down the line until I reached my brush. I pulled it through my short curly hair, which was still damp. It went quickly as I'd given up trying to tame the curls long ago. I put everything back into its home and, wrapped in a soft towel, went into the bedroom to dress.

Luckily, dressing went quickly as well. *Tia* had placed everything in its own home. I pulled on an undershirt, a pullover shirt and sweatpants. Fully dressed, I sat on the bed and breathed for a while. I was tired.

"Corinthia? You up? Did I hear the shower?" *Tia* knocked briefly on the door.

I knew she would come in, and she did. It was nice she always knocked, though. I grabbed my tablet and pressed a button. "Good morning," it said in its tinny little voice.

"Good morning, sweetheart. How did you sleep?" She opened the drapes a little more.

I pressed the icon for 'well' and the machine replied for me.

"Good. Any headache?" She studied me. I shook my head. Migraines from the head injury had proven to be a real deal-breaker with God. Man, they hurt. I had several medications I could take, but they all made me feel like a...zombie, so I was usually in bed for two days, first from the migraine and then from the medicine. Ugh.

She handed me my clogs. "Do you want socks?" She waited expectantly until I shook my head.

"I've got breakfast started, so why don't you head on in and check the toaster for me?"

I nodded and made my way down the hall toward the kitchen. I really liked this little house. I couldn't remember exactly where I'd lived before, but I knew it was *Tia*'s house farther out of town. *Tia* had found this one in the center of town and had paid for it with some of the money from the truck accident that had given me the TBI. Traumatic Brain Injury. She said it was more than two million dollars, and that was good because I would need it to take care of me, for food and clothes and electric.

The toast popped up as I approached it, so I put it on a plate and put in the two pieces of bread that were waiting. Two covered dishes were on the table, and I lifted the lids. One was bacon and scrambled eggs, the other a pile of butter-dripping home fries. My mouth watered.

"Sit down, honey, eat while it's hot. I'll butter those," *Tia* said as she came into the kitchen.

I obeyed her and pressed icons on my tablet. "Thank you… cooking…this," it said.

"You're very welcome, Corinthia. Dig in. But take your pills first."

The food was delicious, and I ate until I was stuffed. *Tia* watched me indulgently as she chewed her own food. "You're gonna have to walk a little extra today if you keep that up," she told me, laughing.

I punched my tablet. "Your fault," I replied.

"So, no therapy today, no visitors. What are you gonna do with yourself all day?"

"Puzzles," I told her.

She nodded. "That's right. You've got three to finish before tomorrow."

I rose and started loading the dishwasher. It was only silverware and the frying pan. Since the injury, *Tia* and I used paper cups, plates and bowls. I was like a bull in a china shop and often broke things with my erratic movements.

After breakfast was cleared, I went to the desktop computer set up on a desk in an anteroom just off the living room. I laid my cane on the floor and switched the machine on. Using the mouse with my stronger right hand, I clicked on the icon and opened the portal my therapist had set up for me. Each week she gave me five strategy puzzles to help me build my cognitive skills. She also encouraged me to play solitaire and other card games whenever I felt like it. Today the puzzle was all about finding hidden items. I did well, quickly locating a key, an apple, three bottles and a pen in the dark, brooding scene these items were hidden in. The second task was a lot harder and it took me the better part of an hour for me to come close to finishing it. I had to put a list of tasks in the order they were typically accomplished. That was on the left-hand side. On the right was a list of items used in these tasks, and they had to be matched and listed in order. Putting things in order was always so hard for me.

I could hear *Tia* in the other room talking on the phone, and I felt unreasonable anger well up in me. I pushed it down but knew I needed medication. Emotions still often went over the top and took me with them.

I slammed my palms on the desktop and lifted myself to my feet. The puzzle was too much. I would go back to it later. I retrieved my cane and went into the kitchen to the cabinet that held my medicines. I opened the cabinet and looked at them. How I hated them. I hated them because they changed my brain chemistry and, when I used them a lot, I didn't even know who I was anymore.

"What do you need, honey?" *Tia* asked as she came into the kitchen. She had her cell phone in one hand. I glanced at it, then at her. I realized my tablet was still on the desk, so I fetched my own cell from my pocket. I awakened it and pressed an icon. "Angry," it said.

"Okay, hon, okay. Here you go." She stepped in front of me and fetched the bottle of Prozac. She opened the bottle and broke a tablet in half. "Here, Corinthia, five milligrams. Are you gonna walk it off too?"

I nodded and took the pill with a juice glass of water. I punched my phone. "Coffee?"

"No, sweetie. You go ahead. Be careful, though. And you need socks and a jacket. It hasn't warmed up yet."

I nodded and went down the hall to fetch these items. Pulling the socks on proved difficult, and I felt anger swell in me again. I persisted and finally, with much huffing and puffing, managed to get them on straight. I slid into my clogs and stood, balancing by holding the back of the chair. I looked up and found *Tia* standing in the doorway watching.

"That's my girl," she said. She came in and kissed my forehead. "Enjoy your coffee, my dear, sweet niece."

CHAPTER THIRTY-EIGHT

Ella

"Are you sure you don't want to come alone?" Jessica asked. I heard the worried note in her voice and felt unreasonably guilty. I hated when she worried about me.

"I just don't feel right leaving her that long," I explained.

"It's because you're afraid she will forget about you, if you're gone too long, aren't you?"

I nodded at Julio. "Yeah, I guess so. Now, tell me all about the anniversary party. Did Brian burn mystery meat on the grill? Did you guys dance?"

She laughed and began telling me about the surprising amount of bourbon that could be consumed in just a few short hours. I listened, making all the right noises, but I was in a bottomless depression that I wasn't sure I could ever climb out of.

After learning from Dr Dorsey that Maddie's speech had been impaired, I felt like my earth was crumbling beneath my feet. How could this vivacious, intelligent woman that I loved be silenced? She had so very much to offer the world, and now she would have no way to express it.

These days, I vacillated between self-pity because I would never hear her speak again and remembering the remarkable ways challenged people like Stephen Hawking had enabled their voices to be heard. The emotional bouncing back and forth was making me feel erratic and out of control most of the time.

Maddie had made great strides since that day she'd awakened, but she still struggled with everyday tasks. I visited her often, but it was absolutely clear that she had forgotten our idyllic stolen days—and nights—in Dothan. I saw no love in her eyes when she looked at me, and each time she did look at me, as just her friend and one-time co-worker, I felt grief well up and burden my heart.

"Are you sure you won't come for Thanksgiving? I promise Mom and Dad are *not* going to be here, in case you were worried about that."

How could I tell my sister that I would be horrible company? That there was no thanksgiving in me anywhere because of the brutal way God had treated Maddie and me? No, I would not be visiting her for Thanksgiving.

"The office is just so shorthanded too. I don't think there's any way I could get away for that long. I also promised Florida that I would stay with Maddie while she heads over into Mississippi to visit her kids before Thanksgiving. She hasn't been for a while, so—"

"Can't Maddie go with her?"

"I don't think she's up for that much traveling just yet. She still goes to therapy two days a week, and she doesn't want to miss that."

Jess sighed. "Okay, sis, but I want it on the record that I am seriously worried about you. You sound really down. Granted, it's justified, but I want to hold your hand and tell you that everything's going to be all right."

"But it's not," I whispered.

"What?"

"It's not going to be all right. I've lost her, and I don't know how to get her back. And I want her back," I replied.

"Ella—"

"They tell you that a head injury often creates a whole new person. They say she might be able to do what she did before, be who she was before, but there will be differences because her brain has to create all new pathways to do what it did before. That's all well and good, and I could deal with that. What I can't deal with is how she has forgotten who I was to her. What she was to me. There's no spark of love, no recognition even when she looks at me, and every time she does look at me…I just die a little."

"Ella, honey, this too shall pass. She has to get better, and when she does, she will remember you and will remember what you two are to one another. I mean, think about what her poor little brain has been through, bounced around like that. It takes time to get healed from that."

I scratched Julio under the chin. "If she is healed. Her mind might never recover. Then what? No medical practice, no life for her…or for me! She and I are linked in so many ways. I can't even imagine life without her. Even now."

"I do understand, hon, you've loved her a long time now. Just give it time, a little longer. Be there for her and try not to get too down about it. Okay?"

I nodded and pressed my face against Julio's soft ears. "Okay."

"What did you say?" She sounded puzzled.

I sat up straight. "I said okay. It's not like I have anything else to do. I just work and visit Maddie and come home. It's not exactly what I had planned for my life, even just a few short months ago."

"Ella, please don't become bitter about this. Maybe you should find a church, talk with a priest."

Anger filled me. "Like that's going to change anything, Jess. I gave up on that a long time ago. Plus, I'm pretty mad at God right now. I'm not so sure He'd want to hear from me."

I heard her gasp. "Ella! You know, maybe He's the one you

should be talking to right now. Talk about how angry you are. It might help."

I let silence reign as I pondered her words. There was a Catholic church just down the street from me. "Maybe I will," I whispered finally.

"I'm sorry, little sis. I just hate this and feel so helpless."

"Oh, I know, Jess." I pulled my phone from my ear and searched my icons. I pressed the one that would let me see her dear face. Within seconds, I was staring at her. She looked tired but so familiar and so comforting. "Oh, Jess," I said.

Her dark blue eyes were so sympathetic. She leaned forward. "You do whatever you need to do to feel better. You know this drill. We've used it so many times in our lives. I have complete faith in you."

I smiled, and I did feel better. "Your pep talks have always done me a world of good, big sis."

She smiled back. "Good."

I took a deep breath and disentangled myself from Julio. "Okay. Going for a walk. There's a church down the street."

She nodded. "Do you know the priest?"

I shrugged. "Not yet."

She grinned at me. "Signing off. I loooove you."

"Love you back." I ended the connection and grabbed my jacket from the coatrack. "Be back soon, Julio. Be a good boy."

My phone rang just as I touched the door. I didn't recognize the number, and sudden fear filled me. Suppose something had happened to Maddie.

"Hello!" I barked into the phone, clutching it tightly, nervously.

"Why, hello, darlin'."

"Who is this?"

"It's Dixie, from the conference. Don't you remember me?"

I certainly remembered her. I thought of soft blond hair and bright, clear blue eyes. A curvy figure.

"Yes Dixie. How are you?"

CHAPTER THIRTY-NINE

Maddie

I loved the walk from my new house to the coffee shop. Especially on a day like today, when the sun was a bright shiny thing calling to me, and the air had a bit of early morning crispness to it. Fall in southern Alabama was pleasant, and I noticed that some big thorny plants with papery flowers—I thought they were called bougainvillea—were still beautifully lush along the walkway. One of my neighbors had a bunch of what *Tia* called blue asters in her yard. They were very pretty flowers.

My therapist, Wendy, said that I should walk every day to help my core muscles stay strong, so I did. My walking had gotten much better during the past month. Though my left arm and leg were still weak, they felt strong today.

I stopped and let the sun heat my face. It felt so good. I only stood there a minute before moving on, my cane making a rattling sound every time it hit the sidewalk. I smelled the coffee when I was still a block away and smiled.

The coffee shop was called Java Stokes, and that was written on the glass doors in big yellow letters. There was a steaming beige coffee cup painted there as well. I shifted my weight onto my cane and pulled open the door.

Stevie looked up from behind the counter. There was a big coffee machine there, and sometimes she disappeared behind it. Stevie made the best coffee.

"Hey Maddie! Good to see you! One hard vanilla latte coming right up."

There was no one in the coffee shop after the morning rush, so I had my choice of tables. I still went to the one in the corner where I always sat. There was more room for my cane there against the wall so it wouldn't stick out and trip someone.

"So, how's your day going?" Stevie asked as she slid into the chair opposite me and placed my coffee on the table.

I fished my phone from my pocket. "Good." I lifted the coffee and pressed two icons. "Better now."

She always gave me a cardboard coffee cup and put a plastic top on it even though the other customers usually used regular ceramic cups. I appreciated that, her looking out for me.

"Good. Therapy must be going well. You're moving well today." She studied me with dark brown eyes. She was a little older than me, and her face had fine wrinkles on her eyes, mouth and neck. She was very pretty, with short graying hair and full lips.

I switched over to talk mode and typed into my phone. "Wendy is a brute. She works me hard."

"Isn't that the point?" She lifted her own cup and took a sip. Foam lingered on her upper lip until her tongue snaked up to lick it off. I watched, mesmerized by this. My own tongue mirrored the movement. I seemed to have no control over it.

"I finally got my kitchen painted. It looks amazing. Now, I should be able to have you over for dinner soon," she said. "I really like living in this town. Houston was fine but so busy. I much prefer the slower pace here in Maypearl."

I smiled and nodded. "I look forward to dinner," the phone said after I typed. I knew she had a small apartment on

Cottonwood Street. I couldn't remember where that was, but she told me she would draw me a map so *Tia* could find it, or she would come and pick me up at my house if I wanted.

The bell on the door jangled, and two elderly ladies entered the café. I'd seen them in there many times, so I waved to them as Stevie rose to take their orders.

"Be right back," she said to me over her shoulder as she walked away. I watched her, wondering at my attraction to her. I was coming to realize that I was a lesbian but didn't quite know what to do with that knowledge. Not that it mattered. Any love life I might have had was a moot point now. I smiled ruefully. Ah, well, I had learned to let go.

I took a deep sip of my coffee and watched as Stevie talked and laughed with the two women. She was a sweet woman, and she did seem to like me, though I was sure only as a friend.

I paused in mid-sip. Maybe she was a lesbian too. It would be nice to have someone to talk to about that. Again, did I care? I finished my sip and frowned at my cup. As if I could talk.

I took in a deep breath and blew out coffee aroma. I could talk. Not like everyone else, but that was okay. Dr Penn, my neurologist, told me that I should never look at what I couldn't do, but what I could.

The two older women seated themselves, and Stevie ducked behind the big coffee machine. It always smelled so good when she made the whooshing sounds back there. After serving them their coffees, she brought me a small plate with something from the big glass box on it. It was a peanut butter cookie, one of my favorites.

"Here you go, sweetie. See if we can get some flesh on those skinny arms and legs." She sat down and watched as I picked at the cookie.

"Hey, has any memory come back?" she asked finally.

I shook my head. I reached for my phone. "There's about two months that are gone, but the rest is come and go. No, it's called hit or miss."

"I'm sort of glad you don't remember the accident. I hear it was awful." Her eyes grew sad.

"I'm not sure why I was there," I typed and waited for the phone to speak. "But they say I was delivering a baby."

"Yes, Lizzie Horten's. Poor little baby boy, never even took the first breath," she muttered sadly. She sat back and lifted her cup.

"They died?" I was horrified. Others had died while I had lived.

She eyed me with some surprise. "Yes, all three of them. And a firefighter."

I stood abruptly, not sure how to handle the rampant emotions raging inside me.

She seemed alarmed. "You didn't know?"

I shook my head and bent to retrieve my cane. I stood and pushed one hand down in a calming gesture. I wanted her to know that telling me was okay. I reached with my right hand and touched her gently on the chin. I smiled for her and then grabbed up my coffee and headed home.

CHAPTER FORTY

Ella

Dixie looked so good, sitting there waiting for me, and I just sort of stood in the restaurant doorway drinking her in for a moment. As if sensing me, she glanced up, saw me and came to hug me.

"I am so glad you could make it," she said, eyes joyful. "I just hate having a meal all alone. It's no fun at all."

I smiled. "Me too," I said.

Part of me felt like I should have gone to the church instead, but I felt helpless, as though I were acting on autopilot. Being here with her felt almost like cheating, even though I knew nothing would happen between us. I still loved Maddie, and that would never change.

After we were seated and our drinks ordered, Dixie leaned forward. "How is your Dr Salas?" she asked. "We were just devastated when we heard the news. I thought my daddy was gonna cry. Is she doing okay?"

"Well, define okay." I cleared my throat. "She's not able to speak yet, but she uses talking apps, so that helps. Physically, she's getting around okay, but she doesn't seem to have any... oh, I don't know. Energy, I guess. Or maybe interest. She just doesn't seem to care about anything the way she used to."

"And her mind? How's her mind?" Her eyes were curious.

I rubbed my forehead, feeling as though a headache was blooming there. "She has a spotty memory, and her language skills are still coming back slowly. She doesn't remember anything about the accident. She knows she is a doctor, but she doesn't remember much about her practice. She doesn't even seem to think about it, not checking in about how her patients are or how the office is operating without her."

"She's not going to be a doctor anymore, is she? That is so fucking awful. I can't even imagine what that must be like, to lose everything in just a few short hours," she said quietly.

"It's pretty damned awful," I whispered.

After a few moments, I was determined to change the subject. "So, have you eaten here before? What's good?" I scanned the menu.

I remembered sharing a meal with Maddie. I remembered how our orders had been identical and how we had laughed about it. I looked up, my universe shifting as Dixie's paleness sat across from me instead of Maddie's exotic darkness.

"I think I'll have a thick, juicy steak," she said, eyes scanning the menu. "I hear they do them up good here."

I nodded. "Sounds good."

Not interested in steak, I ordered the salmon when the server, a young, bearded man, approached bearing two house salads.

"So, have you given any more thought about coming to Dothan for a spell? I'd love to show you my...town." She was enjoying her salad, dipping individual chunks of iceberg lettuce into the house ranch dressing.

The pause was subtle, but I heard it. I needed to nip this in the bud right away, but there was something in me that held back.

"Tell me again why you're in Maypearl? The mother of a student?" I tried to emanate curiosity.

She nodded and chewed until her mouth was empty. "There's this mother of one of our staff members. She lives here in Maypearl. Normally a visiting mother would just hop on a plane in Dothan and be here in forty minutes, but oh no, Missus Branley is scared of flying, so she had to be driven back home."

I was confused. "But wait. How did she get to Dothan?"

Dixie laughed, and I smiled in response. "Guess I should have explained. She took a bus to Dothan two days ago, but the fool woman missed the last bus coming this way today. So what does my daddy do? Instead of driving her home himself, he sends me to do it." She paused. "I'm actually sort of glad."

"You are? Why?" Was I actually flirting with her?

"Well, I got to see you, didn't I?" She smiled sweetly at me, her eyes warm and welcoming.

Our food came, ending what could have been an uncomfortable moment for me. I was torn, wanting Maddie so badly but knowing, with some disappointment, that she was gone from me. A big part of me wanted to disappear with her, but another part wanted to be present, to love, to live life to the fullest.

"Mmm, this is good," Dixie said, sampling her steak.

I looked down at my salmon, resting on a steaming bed of rice and surrounded by bright green steamed broccoli. It wasn't spaghetti marinara. Sorrow swamped me, and I squelched it quickly, taking a huge sip of iced tea.

"How's your salmon?" she asked, looking at my untouched plate. "Hey, are you okay?"

I smiled and nodded, blinking back tears. "Sure, sure. I didn't know they served mac and cheese here." I pointed at her plate with my fork.

She lifted a forkful and savored it seductively. "And it is sooo good!" She speared a few noodles and held her fork out to me. I saw a dare in her gaze and, Lord help me, I took the bite. And immediately regretted it. I almost left. I did not need this kind of conflict in my life. Not at this moment.

The rest of the meal was pleasant and uneventful. I knew Dixie wanted more from me, but I just didn't have it to give. I deflected any further overtures and did not flirt or encourage her. Instead, we talked about her daily life as an administrative assistant to her father, her brother's antics surfing the gay dating scene in Montgomery and about her mother's scare with breast cancer.

"Oh my God, no offense, but I guess that didn't go over well at all with her," I said.

"You know it," she agreed. "The idea of nasty medical stuff bein' done to my mama is so alarming, to me as well as to her. Thank goodness it was benign. I thought she was going to pass out just findin' out she had to have a biopsy. We all held her hand, though, as she pretended to be brave and strong."

She sighed and rolled her eyes. Then she studied me.

"There's something going on with you," she said.

I started to deny it, but she held up a hand to forestall it. She lifted her fork and mashed the remaining piece of chocolate cake that neither of us had eaten.

"You don't have to tell me what it is, but I know it has something to do with Dr Salas. I want to say that I'm really sorry that you're going through a tough time, well, that both of you are. I really hope y'all resolve it soon and that it works out well. If I can help in any way, you just let me know."

I teared up, hearing such heartfelt sentiments from her. I took her free hand between both of mine. "I really appreciate that, Dixie. I think the two of us can be great friends, if that's okay with you."

She nodded and looked away for a moment. "Of course! Girls like us need to stick together," she said brightly as she turned back to me. "Especially in the deep south."

I laughed, filled with relief. "A truer truth has never been spoken."

CHAPTER FORTY-ONE

Maddie

"Why didn't you tell me about the people who died?" I asked her by typing into my phone.

Tia Florida squirmed uncomfortably in her easy chair. "Corinthia, you were in no shape to hear such bad news. We had other things we were dealing with at the time."

I sat down in the recliner next to her. "I just feel bad. I guess I should have died, too," I typed.

Tia dropped the book she'd been reading before my interruption to the floor.

"Corinthia Salas! Don't you dare say such a thing. Ever! People die when it is their time to die. You shame me, and yourself, by pretending you are the Creator and that you make the decisions who should and should not die. Your mother and father raised you better than that."

"Sorry," I typed.

I had forgotten how fatalistic yet devout my family had been. I was beginning to get a whole new idea about that.

"Let's see Mother," I typed.

Tia sat up straighter. "Are you feeling well enough for that? You know she won't recognize you. I told you what her condition is."

I nodded and typed. "Want to remember."

Tia sighed and stood. "Okay. Go get your jacket."

I donned my jacket, and we went outside. I stared longingly at my dark blue Sequoia SUV as we scrambled into *Tia*'s small Toyota pickup. I wasn't driving yet, but we'd gone ahead and repaired my SUV after it was damaged in the explosion. I just needed to get back my self-confidence and I would try. I was looking forward to having that freedom again.

It took us about twenty minutes to get to the home where my mother lived. Try as I might, I had no recollection of this place. The holes in my memory amazed me daily. According to what *Tia* had told me, I used to come here every week. I was looking forward to seeing my *mami*. I hadn't seen her since the accident, and the memories I did have of her were old ones from when I was a child.

The senior center smelled funny inside, like menthol liniment and old food. *Tia* led me past the front desk and down a hallway. We entered a small room. A wizened little lady, with short wavy black-and-gray hair, sat in a chair next to the window. She turned to look at us. I saw it then. I saw the *mami* of my youth, a woman who'd been taller and thinner but with the same dark brown eyes. Emotion choked me, and I gasped. *Tia* pivoted to look at me.

"Corinthia? What's wrong?"

I indicated my mother and then swiped at my streaming eyes.

Tia patted my back. "It's okay, Corinthia. Just let yourself remember. It's all part of the healing."

I nodded and moved closer to my mother. I laid down my cane, knelt at her knees and looked up at her. She looked expectantly at *Tia*.

"Esperida," *Tia* said, nodding respectfully. "You remember Corinthia. I've brought her to see you."

Mami looked at me, and I saw many things swirling in the depths of her chocolate eyes. Finally, recognition settled there. I marveled at that. And at the hand that came up and caressed my cheek. A tear escaped my eyes and traveled a slow, hot path along my cheek. My mother's other hand brushed it away impatiently.

"*No llores,*" she said.

I understood her, and my heart thrilled. I think she had said those words, *no tears,* to me before. Maybe this nightmare *would* end and my memory would even out. Maybe the edges of my past and my recent past would eventually collide and I would be whole again.

"*Pobre bebe, tan triste,*" she said, still studying me.

I looked into her dear, familiar face, and something warm settled inside me. I was very sad, and she sensed it. "*Mami,*" I whispered.

Tia gasped, and it was then I realized that I had spoken. Spoken with my own voice and not a machine.

I said it again. "*Mami.*"

Then, because I could, I said it a little louder. "*Mami.*"

"*Que? Que?*" she asked, scowling.

I pulled her close and hugged her, my cheek against her middle. "*Te amo, Mami,*" I said quietly.

"*Amor, amor,*" she said, patting my back impatiently.

I reared back and looked up at her, realizing that she had gone away. She was looking out the window, her face lit with childish interest. The turn of her head followed a passing car, and I knew she had forgotten that I was there. I slid backward and reached for my cane so I could rise. I looked at *Tia.* She was watching me with a huge amazed smile on her face.

"You spoke. I am so very glad for you, honey. So very glad."

"Me too," I said, and again, the words were unintelligible. Sudden anger seared through me, and my head began to throb. I moaned and held my head.

"Oh, honey. You've pushed yourself too much," *Tia* said rushing to my side. "We need to get you home and down for a nap."

I nodded and allowed her to lead me to the door. My head was hurting so badly that I felt blind.

"Goodbye, Esperida, we will see you soon," she called back to my mother as we stepped into the hall.

CHAPTER FORTY-TWO

Ella

"She spoke today," Florida said as she poured me a glass of iced tea. "And made sense."

"Really?" My heart soared. "What did she say?"

Florida sat in the chair across the table from me. "She was speaking to her mother, and it was in Spanish. Just a few words. Later, when she tried to talk again, in English, it was messed up again."

She pulled open a bag of cookies and passed them to me. I took one. Oatmeal raisin. Yum. "I read an article about that once. That patients with aphasia can often speak another language. One woman came out of a brain injury speaking with a British accent, and she was a French Canadian."

"Wow." Florida was suitably impressed. "Do you think that's what's happening to her?"

I shook my head. "I don't know, but we might tell Dr Penn about it, or at the very least Wendy. Can I have another?" I indicated the cookies.

"Of course," she replied, shoving the bag back toward me.

"How's her moodiness been?"

Florida sighed and scrubbed at her face with both hands. "Lord, Ella, she gets angry, she gets teary-eyed, then decides life isn't worth living. Every single day it's something new."

"Well, at least there's never a dull moment," I said, shrugging.

"Hardy har," she responded. "Are you still coming to stay next week? I'll only be gone two nights."

"Absolutely. I'm glad you'll be taking a few days off. We'll just hang out together. We'll be fine."

"I know, I know. I'm just a worrywart."

"It'll do you a world of good to get away for a few days. And see that new grandbaby." I smiled. "By the way, I expect lots of photos, I hope you know."

We heard Maddie's cane in the hallway.

"Well, hello, sleepyhead," I said when she appeared. Her hair was mussed, and I decided I liked this new shorter look on her. She was still a little too thin, though. She smiled widely at me and opened her tablet as she sank into a chair. "Hi Ella," she typed into the text-to-speech app.

"Your auntie was telling me what a good day you had. Congratulations," I said.

She signed 'thank you' in American Sign Language.

"Oh, Lordy, here you two go again," Florida said, rolling her eyes.

I laughed. Who knew that my ASL lessons in Virginia at my sister's church would come in so handy? Maddie didn't remember everything I'd taught her, but the rudimentary basics along with her tablet were plenty sufficient for us to communicate well.

"How day?" Maddie signed.

"It was good. We only saw about six patients all day, though. You'd think there would be a lot of flu going around this time of year, but that doesn't seem to be the case." I shrugged and spread my hands.

She regarded me thoughtfully, head tilted to one side. Then she bent over her tablet. "Sometimes flu hits in waves. Can happen later in November."

I was taken aback. Wow, girl knew her stuff. "Yeah, yeah, that's true."

"So, we're having Thanksgiving dinner at our house this year. Can you make it?" Florida asked.

"Oh, yeah, sure. Would love that," I said, surprised to be invited. I realized by the mounting joy filling me, that being with Maddie on the holiday, or any day, was exactly where I wanted to be. "Thank you for inviting me!"

"You're family, Ella," Florida said. "Glad you can come, 'cause we'll have plenty. I do like to cook. Now, if you two will excuse me, I've got a TV show to catch up with." She rose and left the kitchen.

"Turkey," Maddie typed. "*Tia* says I love it. I guess I'll find out."

I laughed. "I guess you will."

"My mother doesn't know me all the time," she typed.

"I know, and I'm sorry about that. Alzheimer's is a horrible disease. It takes so many away from their loved ones."

"Like a brain injury?" her tablet asked.

I eyed her closely. Did she remember me? She looked back at me, her eyes and face expressionless. I saw no recognition.

"Yes, like a brain injury," I replied.

"It was like my mother knew I was hurt," she typed. "But she knew me, for just a minute."

I nodded. "I know that meant a lot to you."

"Do you know my life?" she typed.

I sat back in my chair and thought about that. "Well, I know you lived in Puerto Rico and New York. And that a friend had a cat like mine, a Maine Coon—"

"Carla," she typed.

My eyes widened. "You remember that?"

She grimaced and shrugged. "I guess so. What about love?"

I quaked at this new direction. I took a deep breath to fortify myself. "You had a girlfriend in medical school, but I don't remember her name."

She stroked her chin as though in deep thought. Finally, she shook her head. "I thought I might be lesbian," she typed.

I nodded. "Yes, we both are. That's—that's why we became close."

"You worked for me too." She watched me expectantly.

"Yes, yes, I did. I never told anyone about our sexual preferences, though. We kept that to ourselves."

"That a good thing?" She frowned.

"Well, I don't know about that." I laughed shortly. "But it's best for the moment, I suppose."

I stood abruptly, hoping to change the subject. "I'm gonna have more tea, you want some?"

I watched her until she nodded. She was studying me with an oddly speculative glance.

"What? Do I have cookie crumbs on my face?"

She shook her head.

I prepared our glasses of tea and resumed my seat.

"So, what are you thinking for next weekend? I thought maybe a list of movies and a bunch of popcorn."

She sucked on the straw of her adult sippy cup. "Can't wait," she typed. "Can we do horror?"

"Only if you'll let me put nutritional yeast on the popcorn instead of butter." I eyed her challengingly.

"Must love you lots. Agree," she typed.

If only that were so. While I was eternally grateful for the friendship we had developed, I so wished it could be more. But that was okay. Being with Maddie, even this new and different Maddie, was okay.

CHAPTER FORTY-THREE

Maddie

Wind was sweeping my long hair away from my face. I closed my eyes to enjoy the sensation. I also enjoyed the sensation of my thigh muscles contracting regularly as I…skated. I was laughing, talking and holding the hand of someone I dearly loved. We danced around one another, spinning and ducking under one another's arms. I had never been happier and knew that I had to make it last. An elderly woman's face appeared—Esther, Ethel.

I had a smile on my face as I almost woke to full awareness. I kept seeing laughing green eyes, sparkling with joy. They seemed somehow familiar, but I just couldn't remember. I suddenly felt as though I was submerged in water, floating on my back. Hands were holding me up as voices whispered to me. They were whispering a timeline, beginning with my birth back in nineteen seventy-seven and up until the time of my accident. The odd thing was that it stopped at that point.

Though the timeline stopped, it still went farther than I had ever gone before, taking me right up until the explosion. I saw myself as a physician, with my own practice. I saw the faces of my patients, some of whom still visited me today, after I'd been hurt. Until this moment, I hadn't really been able to place them on my own, without help. Now I saw our past interactions and realized how they had been my friends as well as my patients. One of the benefits of a small town. And they still were, at least on their part. I resolved to treat them better in the future. I saw Sandy and Ella, how the three of us were a well-oiled team working together, seeing dozens of patients a day. I saw myself in a car, my car, with Ella. But where were we going?

I stirred restlessly, frustrated at hitting a newly placed brick wall. I wasn't in the car with Ella when it exploded. This had to be another time. I slammed into wakefulness, panting as though I'd run a long race. I banged my weak left fist onto the bed and then spread my fingers wide, flexing them. I grasped the blanket in frustration, knowing that my rage and frustration was wasted emotion. I was finally learning to get some control of the anger, and I waited, seeing if I would have one of my throbbing headaches. I didn't. I actually felt good, thinking very clearly for once.

I sat up and stretched my arms and back. I rose and made the bed, and then, after fetching my cane, started my morning routine. *Tia* was surprised when I appeared in the kitchen.

"Look at you, Miss Early Bird. You must have slept well."

I nodded and gave her a thumbs-up as I seated myself.

"Well, I thought we'd have oatmeal this morning, since it's almost winter and all," she said, busy at the stove.

I chuckled and took my medications with orange juice. I reached for my tablet.

"Packed yet?" I asked her.

"Packed and unpacked twice. And I've finally made a decision." She stood in front of the stove, hands working a dishtowel. "I am only taking enough clothes for two days. The rest of the bag will be for the presents. That's it. One bag."

I frowned. I pressed an icon. "Driving."

She grimaced. "I know, but I just don't want the aggravation."

I snickered and pointed to the stove where the oatmeal was making strange distress sounds and producing loads of steam.

She turned and snatched the pan to an inactive burner. "Sheesh! I don't think it burned, so we're okay." She began dishing up oatmeal for each of us.

"I dreamed," I typed. "There was big wind and I was in love."

Tia stilled and placed the half-full bowl carefully on the counter. "Big wind? What kind of big wind?" Her back was still to me so I couldn't see her face.

I knocked on the table so she would look at me. She turned, and I studied her. Was she hiding something else, something like the deaths of the Horten family and the firefighter? I narrowed my eyes to let her know I was suspicious.

"Oh, stop looking at me like that. I can't imagine what the wind is about, is all. What does it matter? A dream is a dream," she said, turning back to the stove.

I added butter and brown sugar to my oatmeal when she set the bowl in front of me. "The wind was skating, I think," I typed. "Don't know who I was in love with."

She seated herself and added butter and milk to her bowl. "Skating sounds like fun. Did you know there's a roller rink in Mobile, just off Central? Is that where you were in your dream?"

I shook my head in the negative. "This one had cartoons."

She paused, spoon halfway to her lips. "Cartoons? I've never heard of a skating rink with cartoons."

I shrugged and dug in. We were mostly silent for the rest of the meal, each lost in our own thoughts. I knew *Tia* was thinking about her upcoming trip, and I was trying to decide which horror movies to reserve on my Netflix list. I helped her load the dishwasher, and then I went to my room to get ready for therapy.

Tia often went to get groceries when she dropped me off for therapy. Sometimes she went to the library to return or get books. She was a big reader. I hadn't remembered that, so it was almost like I was getting to know *Tia* all over again.

Wendy was in a good mood. We spent a good bit of time talking today. I told her about the visit with my mother, about the talking.

"Wow, that's wonderful!" she said, straightening her shirt collar. "*Se habla español?*"

"*Sí, hablo español. Es lo que yo he nacido para*—" I stopped, realizing that I was talking again. Without my machine.

"*Ta bueno!*" she exclaimed, clapping her hands.

I grinned but realized I had a small problem. I had forgotten most of my Spanish. Whether from disuse or the TBI, I wasn't sure, but most of it was gone.

CHAPTER FORTY-FOUR

Ella

"I'll be back tomorrow to feed you. Maybe I'll bring Maddie to see you. Would you like that? I bet you've been missing her," I told Julio as I zipped my bag.

I looked toward the bed and remembered how Julio had settled on Maddie's hip that final night we were together. "You don't have anyone to claw these days," I added.

My eyes sped toward the bathroom mirror. The lipstick heart I had drawn for Maddie was still there. I couldn't bear to wipe it away.

I sat on the bed and wrapped my arms about myself. "I had such plans for us, Julio. I mean, I was going to try to cook dinner for us every night. I was going to take her to Jess's for the anniversary party. I really wanted her to meet Jess and… and Barbie. And Westie, oh, she would have loved Westie and Westie her." Julio jumped on the bed and butted me with his head.

Tears swelled and fell onto my folded hands. They were hot, and I massaged the moisture into my skin with my thumbs until it disappeared. I had to be strong. I had to be Maddie's friend and help her through this time of healing. She had a lot of friends that were helping her, but I was the one who knew her best.

I stood and smoothed down my shirt. "Okay, I'm gonna leave the timer on so you can have three hours of TV each evening. No more than that. Those shows will rot your brain," I told him as I leaned across the bed to kiss his head. "Be a good boy."

I carried my overnight bag to the front and grabbed my pocketbook. I took one final look around and stepped out into the bright fall sunshine.

Florida opened the door when I got to her house. "Hey girl. What are you doing here so early?"

"Ah, Dr McLean had a dentist appointment. I thought I'd let you get an earlier start."

"Child, you are so sweet." She drew me into a big, comfy hug, and I relaxed into it, enjoying it fully. "Let's go in and I'll get my things."

"Where's Maddie?" I asked, looking around the living room.

"Down at the coffee shop. Getting her daily walking therapy and caffeine boost."

"Ah yes, forgot about that. Maybe I'll walk down and walk her home. Do you need any help loading the car?"

"Oh no, I just have the one bag. If you can go get her, I'll get myself ready, and I'll say goodbye to her when y'all get back." She started to turn away and then returned, fishing keys from her pocket. "Maddie has her own set, but I'd feel better if you took my spare house keys. Just so I won't worry."

I took the keys from her and then held her by the shoulders and looked her in the eye. "Please. I got this. You go have a great time with your other family. We'll be fine, okay?"

She nodded and dropped her eyes. "I should tell you…she's been dreaming."

"About?"

"I think memory stuff, like skating and love. I don't know if she's just dreaming or remembering. I don't know how these will affect her. I guess that's why I'm worried."

I fell into thought. Could she be remembering our trip to Dothan? "I…I think it's probably a good thing, but I'll be on extra alert, just in case, okay?"

Florida nodded and patted my hands. "Go. Fetch her home, and I'll go get ready."

As I walked the half-dozen blocks to the Java Stokes, I breathed in the fragrant bouquet of smells swirling around me. One thing about southern Alabama, when almost everywhere else in the country north of us was in a frigid stasis, we were getting our second wave of flowering growth. A temperature in the midseventies seemed to be perfect to nudge out a new round of blooming color. An ocean breeze wafted across me, and I inhaled the oxygen-saturated air. I hummed to myself as I walked along, thinking how great it would be if she really was remembering something. Maybe we could talk this weekend, and I could get some idea what was going on in her dreams.

I rounded the corner, and the smell of fresh roasted coffee assailed me. Oh yeah, I was definitely going to grab a coffee for the walk home. I reached for the door handle, and that was when I saw them. They were sitting at a table in the corner, in a mostly deserted coffee shop. I wasn't sure who the woman was, but she wore a green apron over her clothing, so I assumed she worked there. And she was touching my Maddie.

They were sitting side by side, and I had a perfect vantage point from my stance outside the front doors. The woman had one hand on Maddie's cheek, caressing it. They were smiling tenderly at one another, and sorrow swamped me. Had Maddie found a new love? Was this who she was dreaming about? I bit my bottom lip to keep from crying—or crying out. I stood there a long time, too long, trying to deal with what I was seeing. Finally, the woman stood and moved back to the counter to speak with the young couple seated on the other side of the room. I observed as Maddie watched her walk away. What was she thinking about this woman?

I took a deep breath and gritted my teeth. Once inside, I walked straight to Maddie with a big smile.

"Ella!" she signed and rose to hug me. She pulled the woman's chair back and pushed me into it. "Why here?" she signed.

"I came to get you," I said, trying to be cheerful. "I got off early, and *Tia* Florida told me you were here. I came to walk you home."

"Cool!" she signed and then gave me a thumbs-up gesture.

I looked at her coffee cup. "You need a refill? Thought I'd get one too."

She nodded, and I took her cup to the front counter. The woman was behind the counter. She was very attractive, and my heart ached. I was so very close to sobbing, but I swallowed the tears.

She smiled at me, and I extended my hand. "Hi. I'm Ella, Maddie's friend."

"Oh. Hello! Good to meet you. I'm Stevie Phelps, owner of this here java joint."

Her upbeat personality was contagious, and I couldn't help feeling some semblance of relief that if I had to lose Maddie's love, it would be to someone good and positive.

CHAPTER FORTY-FIVE

Maddie

"I think they're cannibals," I typed when Ella came back from the bathroom.

"Really? Why do you think that?"

"Kids," I signed.

"What about the kids?" She looked at the television and squinted as if she could glean something from the paused movie.

"Weird," I signed. "Around father."

"Ahh, so you think he was forcing them to eat people?"

I nodded. "Family ritual," I typed.

She curled up next to me on the sofa. We had both gotten into our snuggly pajamas, and we had a blanket over our legs as we watched horror movies on the big TV in the den. It was fun, and I loved being so close to her. She had this really wonderful smell, kind of earthy and woody. I really liked the way she smelled.

"Okay, go," she urged.

I pressed the pause button and the action resumed. Sure enough, within half an hour, the family was serving up human stew, with an ear floating on top. The mother was serving it to her two daughters hesitantly, like it was against her will.

"Ewwww," Ella said. "That is so gross." She looked at the slice of pizza on the plate she held in her hand. She placed the plate on the coffee table.

I nodded in agreement and made a face. "Like *Texas Chainsaw*," I typed.

"No, *Chainsaw* would have to be worse," she argued. "I mean, they did skin lampshades and stuff in those movies in addition to eating the people."

"True," I typed.

We watched until the end, when the children cooked dear old dad. I muted the music playing over the ending credits then looked at Ella. "Cool," I typed.

"Sick," she said, nudging me with one hand. She rose. "I'm gonna get another beer. Are you sure it's okay if you have another?"

"Didn't say anything about drink," I typed. "Just no fall."

She nodded and slid into the kitchen on stocking feet. I found myself hoping *she* wouldn't fall. I never walked in stocking feet anymore. It was bare feet or wide-based clogs for me these days as I still had balance issues. I pulled the blanket close, my mind wandering aimlessly. I was thinking about *Tia* driving into south Mississippi. I wondered what her children looked like these days. Last time I'd seen them, they'd still been in high school. I realized that although I expected to bring their visages to light in my mind, it wasn't happening. Damned memory blocks.

Ella handed me a cold beer and crawled back into the pocket of warmth we'd created in the blankets. I read the label on the beer bottle. It was a light beer, lower in calories. A good thing, I supposed. I took a sip and held the bubbly goodness in my mouth for a long while. I enjoyed the popping sensations. I swallowed when most of the fizz had left.

"Glad I can still read," I typed.

"Hmm? Oh yeah, me too. You're really making some remarkable strides these days. Maybe by the time you get your words back, your memory will be all filled in." She studied me closely, and I saw that speculative look in her eyes, an expression that she often wore when studying me.

I nodded and smiled, miming my agreement for the possibility. An idea occurred to me. "Will you still hang out when well?" I typed.

"Hang out with you? Of course, you're my bestest bud." She grinned at me but turned her gaze away. I didn't know what that meant. I still sucked at what *Tia* called nuance.

"Okay, my turn to pick." She took the remote and started scrolling through movies. "Let's see. I'll check the new ones. Maybe there's some new scary ones we haven't seen...Oh my God. Look what's just been added."

I looked at the screen, but it was just a lot of colors.

"This is my all-time favorite. You, my dear, are gonna loooove it. It's called *The Incredibles*."

I nodded and sat back as the movie started. I covered my eyes as the strobing purple and blue lights filled the huge screen, so Ella fast-forwarded with the remote. Lights flashing always made my head feel weird. One time a stoplight changing had given me a sick migraine. When I finally looked at the screen again, there was a car chase. A superhero rescued a cat and stopped a bank robbery. There was a big fight. An annoying kid. A female superhero. Then the superhero in regular clothes—a strangely shaped cartoon man—was having trouble fitting in his car. It was interesting, and the animation was amazingly real.

I sat up suddenly. I knew these people. Where had I seen them before? That bright shock of orange hair. I should know that, should remember that.

"I think I've seen this," I typed.

"Really?" She seemed surprised. "I thought...well, before, you said you hadn't seen it."

I continued to be mesmerized by the screen, so I couldn't answer her right away. Instead, I pulled the blanket higher so that only my eyes were out, raptly following the action on the screen. It was a good story, and I was enjoying the bright colors and well-formed action. I found myself laughing along with Ella during comical scenes. I liked Edna the best.

I looked over at her once and realized how good this felt. I was having the best time I'd had since the accident. Ella was someone who I could relax with. I knew that she wouldn't ask too much of me, thereby making me feel inadequate, nor would she brush me and my slow, sometimes incomprehensible thoughts aside. She really was a good friend. She returned my glance and winked at me. She extended her beer bottle and clinked it against mine in a toast celebrating life and our time together.

CHAPTER FORTY-SIX

Ella

"Will you take me to cemetery?" Maddie typed the next morning as we were finishing breakfast. We'd both had a lot of beer and pizza the night before, so we were waking up very slowly. It was close to midday already.

I frowned at her, raising one eyebrow. "Yes? What cemetery do you want to go to?"

She shrugged in answer.

"I guess you mean the one here in town?" I studied her, trying to understand why the cemetery was important.

"Horten," she spelled out the name in sign, using her fingers with some difficulty.

"Good signing, Maddie!" I fell silent for a brief moment. "Yes, Maddie, I will certainly take you to the cemetery. Shall we pick up some flowers on the way?"

She nodded and rose to clear the table.

Saturday in Maypearl was always my favorite day there. The farmer's market was set up in the grassy center of town, although this was the short slower season before the vegetables got their renewed winter growth, so the pickings were slim. We parked and then walked in, taking our time. We stopped at Stacy Evan's flower booth and bought a sizeable bouquet.

Today the square was full of loitering townsfolk, catching some rays and enjoying this beautiful day. We slowed as we passed them, so Maddie could return the many waves sent her way. I actually had to sit and wait once so a group of her former patients could come over and visit with her for a long chat. I finally realized they were exhausting her, so I soon shooed them away, citing an appointment as an excuse.

"Want to go by and see Julio after?" I asked Maddie as we pulled out of the parking space and set off onto a stretch of open road. "I need to feed him his wet food or he won't speak to me for a week."

She laughed as she typed. "Yes, really want see him."

I saw the steeple of the God's Gold Methodist Church just ahead. I slowed and pulled off and into the first turn into the labyrinthine cemetery. I jostled my memory, trying to remember exactly where the Horten family had been buried. I drove slowly, making turns that would lead me closer to the back of the church. I recognized a tree finally and pulled over and parked on the side of the road.

"I think this is it, Maddie. Are you ready?" I studied her face, trying to determine her emotional state. As happened so often since her injury, her face was a blank slate.

She nodded and lifted her cane. It was a short walk to the fresh graves that were just now being covered by lush, creeping grass. The headstone had been placed already, and we stood at the foot of the graves, reading it.

"They named him?" she typed into her phone.

"Lizzie's sister did. She said Lizzie had chosen Carter Darwin for him."

"It's a nice name," she typed. "Solid."

I turned to her to agree and saw that tears were streaming along her lean cheeks.

"Ah Maddie. Don't cry, sweetie."

"Should have died," she typed. "They should live. Baby should live."

I didn't know how to respond to that. What could I say? Slowly, I began talking, just sharing what was in my heart.

"You know, Maddie. The bad things in life are not our choices to make. They just happen. I personally believe everything happens for a reason. I remember how angry I was after your injury. I even blamed Lizzie for being pregnant."

She gasped and lifted wide eyes to me. I waved her indignation away.

"Believe me, I now realize how wrong and…stupid that was. I have learned during the past thirty-odd years that life is not so much about what happens to us but that it's how we react to it that matters. It's like there's a tally, some kind of heavenly chart that marks how we react to whatever is thrown our way." I shook my head. "It's not that I'm religious or even that I believe in God. He may just be a social construct made by man to meet some deep-seated need. The point is we can't know for sure about God, so we act on faith. With that in mind, and the golden rule of do unto others firmly ensconced in our psyche, why not act as though the tally, the score, *is* being kept? What harm can it do? The result is still reacting in a good, wise and honorable way. There's no downside to that."

"Why?" she signed.

"Why am I telling you this? Well, it hurts me to hear you say you should have died. No, you shouldn't have, and I do believe there's a reason for that. Think about how we, all of us here in Maypearl, would be devastated by your death. The townsfolk see how hard you are working to recover, and maybe it gives them a little faith in themselves and in a universe that rewards persistence and survival. Maybe you inspire other wounded people to strive to come back as far as they can. We can't always know specifics, but by living our lives in such a way, we can hope that what and who we are radiates out a little bit beyond ourselves."

Silence settled around us until a black grackle rasped in a nearby tree. A cricket sang in a pile of brush, and I could hear the distant traffic on the highway. I looked at all the headstones surrounding us. Being here was somewhat surrealistic. Had we joined the dead?

"The funeral was beautiful," I said. "Sandy and I went to both funerals since we knew you couldn't be there."

"Thank you," she signed.

Maddie took the bouquet of flowers from my hands and stepped forward to lay them in the center of the wide, three-person headstone. She bowed her head a brief moment before stepping back to stand beside me. Her hand found mine and grasped it. I entwined my fingers with hers, and we stayed there a long time, the sun slanting hot and heavy on our backs.

CHAPTER FORTY-SEVEN

Maddie

"Yes. Weird dreams too," I typed into my tablet.

We were in Dave's Diner having spaghetti and crusty Italian bread.

After leaving the cemetery, we'd gone to Ella's cute little apartment where I got to play with Julio. I loved that cat. I sort of remembered him from before. Ella said the Julio and I had only met a few times, though.

"What were they about?" Ella asked. She was watching me with curiosity.

I wiped my hands and responded with my tablet. "I dreamed I was skating. I guess roller-skating."

She tilted her head to one side as she chewed reflectively. "When was the last time you skated?"

I shrugged. "Never," I signed.

She looked at her plate. "So, where do you think this is coming from?" she asked quietly.

I sipped through my straw as I wondered that myself. The dream had seemed so real, like a memory. I knew, from what *Tia* had told me that I hadn't been to Mobile any time lately, and

"Hmph!" Sandy said before waving for the server. She approached and greeted Sandy with a warm hug.

"You'll be wanting your regular coffee and sweet bun, I suppose," she said, scribbling on her notepad.

"That'd be lovely, Annamarie. You girls don't mind if I join you, do you?"

"Of course not," Ella said. "Can we have sweet rolls and coffee all around?" she asked Annamarie.

"Sure thing," she said, scurrying off.

Sandy took my hand and patted it. "How are you doing, sweetie? I couldn't come by last week because Michael had the flu and he and his mama were staying with Bob and me so Bob could look after him during the day. I didn't want to bring it to you and your house."

"*Tia* told me you called," I typed.

"Well, of course. I wanted to check on you and let y'all know why I wasn't coming around."

"Is Michael better?" Ella asked. "He got that antivirus from Dr McLean, didn't he?"

Sandy nodded her thanks as Annamarie placed a steaming cup of coffee in front of her. "Yes, and it knocked it out in about three days. Amazing stuff they can do with medicines these days."

She turned her attention to me. "So, what are y'all doing out and about? Is Florida still in Meridian?"

I nodded. "Be home tomorrow night," I typed.

"I bet she's having a great time with all those kids and grandkids."

"You bet," Ella answered. "She's supposed to be sending me pictures, but I guess she's been too busy. I'll text her tonight and see how everything's going."

Annamarie brought over a plate with three warm, sticky pecan rolls to the table. We reached for them as one and then laughed together as we lifted them to our lips.

"Ohh, life is good," Sandy said, mouth full.

I had to agree.

CHAPTER FORTY-EIGHT

Ella

Alone in the guest room bed Saturday night, I lay very still, filled with fear. Maddie was remembering a lot, and she was looking to me, as her best friend, to fill in the gaps for her.

I clenched my hands and faced my fear head-on. Did I want her to remember us? Would the knowledge of what we had been to one another please her or confuse her? Would she think I'd lied to her for not telling her about us right away?

I think if everyone had known we were a couple...if we'd had time to make our relationship known to family and friends... Well, it would have been very different. I would have had a status in her life, and people would have understood that. I would have been allowed—it would be expected—that I would coordinate her care. Our relationship had been so new when the accident happened—

I tossed the blankets restlessly. I thought of Maddie in the next room and imagined that she was whole and loved me back the way I loved her. I remembered the few short days we'd had as lovers, how we'd become one so very easily. I still felt that connection to her even though she didn't realize it. Or feel the same way toward me.

But if she remembered... I curled on my side in a fetal position. Maybe going on the way we were was best for her. If what Dr Dorsey said was true, her emotions had been damaged by the head injury. Maybe she wasn't capable of more, and I shouldn't wish that on her. I could do it, I thought. I could spend the rest of my life by her side as her friend, if that was what she needed, if it was what was best for her.

Dixie's face appeared in my mind, and I wondered at that before pushing it away. Dixie could never provide what I really needed, which was Maddie. Maddie, even this damaged shell of who my Maddie had been, was what I wanted and needed.

But what to tell her when she queried me the way she had been? Did I continue to evade and lie, or should I open up, be truthful and let the chips fall where they would?

But suppose I told her the truth and then she felt beholden to be with me. I remembered seeing her with Stevie. Did she want Stevie as a romantic partner? Could I step in the way of that?

I buried my face in the pillow. "Hell yes, I could. Maddie was mine and always will be," I whispered.

"Maybe having me around is a good talisman," I told Maddie the next morning at breakfast. "You haven't had one single headache since I've been here."

"Thank you," she signed, her mouth full of pancake.

This Maddie was a bit more childlike than the other Maddie. The original Maddie had been more careful, more circumspect. This new Maddie was more candid, more immediate in some ways. And though she was more relaxed about life, I'd seen flashes of the keen intellect she'd had before. I was fast becoming used to this new normal. Now, I wondered if Maddie would ever become comfortable with it. She did seem calmer and more accepting than she'd been right after the injury.

"Stop staring," she typed into her tablet.

"Oops, sorry," I said, grimacing. "Got lost in thought."

"About me?" She watched me expectantly.

"Yeah, sorta."

"Good thoughts?" she typed.

I raised one eyebrow. "Fish for compliments much? Of course good thoughts."

We ate in silence.

"Maddie?"

She looked up.

"If you could change one thing in your life, what would it be?"

She pondered this a long beat. "Today, it would be driving," she typed.

I was flummoxed. Nothing about not having the TBI, or being a doctor again. But driving.

"Driving? That's it?"

"Yes," she typed. "Have a car."

"I know you do, sweetie. Do you want me to teach you how to drive again?"

"Yes," she signed eagerly. "Yes."

I laughed. "Okay. Do you know where your keys are?"

She nodded and leapt to her feet, hurriedly clearing the table. She disappeared down the hall, her cane beating a staccato tattoo on the wooden floor. Moments later, we were sitting in her SUV with me in the driver's seat.

"We'll go to the mall and drive around there. It should be pretty deserted on a Sunday morning." I checked the mirrors and then backed out onto Central. I glanced at Maddie. I could tell she was as nervous as she was excited. We drove through the quiet center of town and farther along Central until we came to the Four Winds Mall, which was the lifeblood of our small town. Everything happened there: our movie theater, food court, gamer hangouts and just about all shopping. Well, besides groceries. It all happened in this one huge complex. I drove us around to the side and put the car in park.

I looked at Maddie, and I could feel my own excitement welling up. "This is so cool," I said. "Are you ready?"

She looked at me with shining eyes and signed "yes" as she scrambled from the passenger seat. I moved her cane over and took her place, and then I watched as she got into the driver's seat and buckled in. She savored the moment a few brief seconds before checking the mirrors and taking it out of parking gear. The car rolled forward and she stomped the brake too hard, causing us both to burst out laughing. She drove forward again and then drove slowly around the perimeter of the parking lot.

"You're doing really well, Maddie. I guess it is like falling off a horse. You just need to get into the saddle again."

She snickered yet kept her eyes in front of her and continued to drive. By the end of almost an hour of driving, she was exhausted, I could tell. She had spent the past fifteen minutes weaving in and out of parked cars and I could see her hands trembling.

"Maddie? I know you are loving this, but we need to stop. Your Aunt Florida will be home soon, and if she sees all those dirty cups and silver we left in the sink, she'll have my hide," I said, keeping my tone light.

Maddie nodded and pulled to one side and put the SUV in park. I touched her forearm. "You did a fantastic job," I told her.

She covered my hand with hers and smiled at me, thrilling my heart.

I switched places with her and headed back to her house. She dozed off before we were halfway there.

CHAPTER FORTY-NINE

Maddie

I fell into my chest and lay across the red, beating muscle of my heart. I think I was dreaming...or maybe remembering, though a part of me knew I would be dead if I had actually cracked my chest open.

I could feel the rhythm of the pulse beneath me. As I lay there, lost in the rhythmic beat, lights from the heart rose and surrounded me. Their bright warmth enclosed me and buoyed me up onto a new warmth of the flesh. They brought me into a new kind of heat, actually hotter than my skin. The lights blinded me, but they diminished enough to allow me to see the dear face under me. I had my fingers entangled in thick blond hair, and my body ached with the pleasure suffusing me. I pressed my lips against hers again, and our tongues danced a minuet as I took and gave and she took and gave. I brought up my knee, and my thigh found warm, wet delights. I pressed myself, my very center, into the thigh of the woman below me.

My lips eventually found the smooth, fragrant skin of her neck. As I traveled lower, across the gentle rise of her breast, the heat of the lights increased until they filled me, waned then filled me again with this heat. I felt that I would explode soon if the lights of the heart continued. I was relishing the heat, though, feeling the energizing gift of that intense power. I could accomplish anything with these beautiful, glowing blue-green eyes looking at me.

I awoke abruptly, eyes snapping open and seeing only darkness. The glow of the streetlights penetrated my vision, and I realized I was in my bedroom. I glanced at the digital clock and saw it was two fifteen in the morning. I relaxed into the bed, hugging my pillow close. I went over the dream in my mind. There was something I was missing, but I couldn't quite put my finger on it. The woman in the dream…I recognized her. That familiar scent, those beautiful green eyes. I suddenly knew what I had been overlooking. It was Ella. I loved Ella, loved her with every part of my being. A life without her in it would not be worth living.

What should I do with this knowledge? It didn't matter that she had been my friend through the insanity of my brain injury; being in a relationship with a disabled person was a whole different thing. Funny—I realized that I had never asked if she was *in* a relationship. I had seen no evidence of it at her apartment, but that didn't mean she wasn't seeing someone. My heart lurched painfully. I turned and grabbed my phone from its charging cradle on my nightstand. I found Ella's icon and pressed it. The message application opened and I typed a message. "Are you seeing anyone?" I wrote. "Are you in a relationship?"

I pushed send and then replaced the phone. I knew she wouldn't answer tonight. She had to be sleeping. I was just turning over to try to go back to sleep myself when a soft chime sounded. It was her. My Ella.

"You're awake!" I typed. "Don't you have work?"

"Yep, just couldn't sleep. Y R U awake?"

"Dreaming, woke up," I answered.

"R U OK? Headache?"

"No. Just wondered if U R in a relationship," I answered.

After a long pause, she responded. "I was. Ended, sort of."

"Do U still C her?" I curled on my side and nestled myself, and the phone, into the blankets.

"Sometimes but it's not like it was before," she responded.

"Do U wish it was?"

Another long pause.

"I really don't know. It's good the way it is now. Better all around, I guess. Why R U thinking abt this?"

"I don't know," I answered finally. "I had this dream and…" I stayed my finger. There was so much I wanted to say and this …typing…was so frustrating.

"Look, go to sleep. I need to sleep 2."

"Will I C U tomorrow?" I asked.

"Sure, I will come by after work. Julio says night night."

I smiled into the phone, even though she couldn't see me. "Night, night Julio."

After signing off, I lay there in the dark, listening to the night sounds all around me. I imagined still being friends with Ella and not revealing my love until she was ready. Or maybe until I was ready. And then I imagined so much more. I eventually drifted off to sleep.

CHAPTER FIFTY

Ella

"Oh man! That was good, Florida, but you don't have to feed me every time I come over."

"Bah! You're family, Ella. Thought you knew that." She waved my protestations aside. I helped her clear the table and put the leftover roast and vegetables in the refrigerator.

While wiping off the table, I glanced at Maddie, who was kneeling by the coffee table. "She's still at it, huh?"

Florida laughed. "Yes. I'm not sure how we'll ever get it away from her. We're lucky that we got her to eat."

The cousins had sent Maddie a magnetic building set, and she had been entranced with it since Florida had unpacked it earlier that morning. She'd shown it to me as soon as I had arrived, after giving me an uncharacteristic kiss on the cheek along with my usual hug. During dinner, she had been distracted, glancing often at the coffee table and the shiny, colorful building blocks atop it.

I sat on the sofa and watched her build. Though there was not much building going on. She seemed fascinated at the repel aspects of the magnetized blocks, pulling them together and then letting them shoot apart. I watched her, and though one could say she was playing as a child would, she held herself regally and her face was very serious. I could see her trying to figure out the physics of the magnetism.

"If the two ends are the same, they repel," I said. "If they are different, positive and negative, they attract," I explained.

Florida came in and kissed Maddie on the top of the head. "Okay, kiddos, off to my room to read. Y'all behave and no fighting over the toys." She chuckled at her joke.

I stood. "Guess I'd better be getting home so you guys can turn in."

Florida waved me back down onto the sofa. "Stay, play. She loves having you here."

I resumed my seat on the sofa. I slipped off my shoes and sat back, legs curled under me, still watching her. She was such a beautiful woman. I'd thought so since the day we'd met. That seemed like so long ago, when actually it had been only a little more than two years ago.

She must have felt me watching her, for she looked up and flashed me that adorable smile I'd become so familiar with before her accident. I was glad to see it had returned.

She pulled her tablet closer. "You're watching me again," she typed.

"It's become one of my favorite hobbies," I joked. "It's like watching paint dry."

It took her almost half a minute, but she got it and laughed, nodding her agreement. When she sobered, she looked at me. Really looked at me, and my old hunger for her burst forth. I tried to squelch it, but I was sure she heard my swift intake of breath and saw my cheeks flush with wanting her. I started to say something smart—something to laugh off the attraction—but my phone vibrated in my pocket. I averted my gaze, glad to have a distraction. The caller ID said that it was Dixie. I let it go to voice mail.

"Who was it?" Maddie typed.

"Just Dixie," I responded.

Maddie turned back to her magnetic blocks as I tried to shake off what I was feeling for her.